I0685370

Majician's

Journey

Majician's Journey

David Scherer

Fourth Muse Books

Copyright © 2010 David Scherer
Edited By Gregory D'Orazio
All Rights Reserved. Published by Fourth Muse Books.

The text for this book is set in Arial Narrow

If you purchased this book without a cover it has been reported
as "Damaged or Stolen" by the retailer and neither the
Publisher nor the Author have received payment.

This is a work of fiction. Names, characters, places and
incidents are either the product of the author's imagination or
are used fictitiously, and any resemblance to any persons,
living or dead, business establishments, events, or locales, is
entirely coincidental.

First Edition
10 9 8 7 6 5 4 3 2 1

ISBN-13: 978-0615436227
ISBN-10: 0615436226

For every author who has inspired one child to read, and for all those who influenced my style. I hope to one day be able to attest to the same feats.

For Mildred "Grammy" Bungard, William "Pappy" Nodd, Harriett "Grandma" Celar: The three saddest and scariest moments of my life were when I lost you. Thank you for everything you've taught me. I would have never started writing without you. I just wish you were here to share this with me now.

For Greg Summers, you will be missed greatly by your friends and family, and your loss is met with grief. Thank you for all the kindness you've given to all of us. Your deeds will not be forgotten, your memory never lost, and your heart grows on in all of us. May God rest your soul.

Gathering

His hand was warm as he spread his fingers across my left shoulder blade. I kept trying to talk myself out of this. I'd half-expected Mica to do just that, talk us all out of these stupid marks, but he thought it was a good idea too. Of course the whole thing was just a stupid teenaged idea, let's get a tattoo, brothers forever, that deal. Since even Kai couldn't charm a tattoo place into inking us, and none of us were brave enough to do it ourselves, we decided to use majick.

"Just do it Kai." I gritted my teeth together, I heard their grinding in my head as Kai spoke softly, slowly, trance-like.

1

In battle and through death
Sworn to you I am
Marked you by me
Bound eternal

I expected to feel pain, like getting a real tattoo. There was none. As Kai spoke, I could feel something warmer than his hand tracing across my skin as the majick flowed through his palm. The sensation mostly made me feel uncomfortable.

When Kai was done speaking and I could no longer feel the majick brushing against my shoulder, I stood up, and looked at the mark in the mirror, it was a triquetra with a circle going through it. It looked almost like it had been drawn on with a deft hand with a permanent marker, the black of the mark was so deep and pure. The tattoo appeared to sit on top of my skin, like it were floating there, on the surface of my skin.

Then it was Mica's turn. He sat backwards on the chair in my room, and crossed his arms across the back, leaning his head on them just as I had. "I'm ready when you are Mattes."

"Your shirt?" I said, moving to stand behind him, putting my own back on. He pulled it over his head and laid the bundled shirt in his lap, leaning over the back of the chair as before.

I spread my fingers over his left shoulder blade. Mica's skin was warm under my fingers. I focused on the majick in my core and spoke in the same soft, slow, trance-like tone as Kai. I could feel the majick flowing down my arm. I could feel it dancing from my palm and tracing the mark over his shoulder. The muscles in his shoulders tensed briefly, when the spell started, but he relaxed almost immediately.

"Kai, you're up." Mica said, standing after I'd finished. He inspected himself in the mirror and pulled his shirt back over his head, fishing his arms through the sleeves.

Almost two years have passed since the night we tattooed ourselves, the one year anniversary of our getting along. Maerik, my teacher, found me huddled in an alley a few miles from my suburban home. It was dark, cold, and rainy, and I was eating stolen food from the store around the corner. My parents had thrown me out after I'd accidentally used majick to set the couch on fire during an argument with them about curfew.

They hated me from then on, refusing to call a satanic

3

devil-worshiper their son. I was so glad when Maerik came and took me home. I had warm clothes, a dry bed, and all the food a thirteen-year-old boy could possibly want. It was here I would spend the next three years learning to control my majick, and learning to put it to use helping people.

It was here that I met Mica and Kai at one of the leadership summits the heads of our coven, Loedium Fertum, took turns hosting. They hated each other, but I seemed to get along with both of them well. After a few months of hanging out, playing the occasional pickup game of soccer, I was sick and tired of their fighting. If the two of them weren't patronizing each other, or making fun of each other, they were grappling around on the ground, trying to mess up the others face as much as possible before anyone could pull them apart. I told them I wasn't going to get in between them anymore and that if they wanted to fight like animals, fine, but I wasn't having any part of it. It took some getting used to, but they were able to be cordial, and eventually became friends.

A year later we sat in my room, probably making the biggest mistake of our lives, tattooing each other with majick. Now I sit here on my bed, thinking back over the past three years, remembering all the good things, and all the bad. I'm so grateful for Maerik, he's the only person who ever really treated me like a son, not an obligation. His hard exterior will fool almost anyone, but in his eyes you can see the kindness that overflows there.

I bent over and tugged on my other shoe, pulling the laces tight and tying them. I grabbed my white robe with the Seal of Solomon embroidered in gold over my right breast and pulled it over my head. I stuffed my arms down the sleeves and checked myself in the mirror.

When I was satisfied my hair was neat enough, I grabbed a small bundle of cloth from the top shelf of my wardrobe, and stuffed it in my pocket. It was my crystal, tonight I receive my Rites, and could wear the crystal around my neck. We used them to focus and store our strongest majick. This would be my final coven meeting as a student.

Discovery

We pulled off the main road onto a rugged side road, you know the type: riddled with potholes and unkempt because it isn't as important. Well! The seats in Maerik's car were not very comfortable, so my backside begs to differ.

From the side road we pulled off onto yet another road, which was a dirt road, and surprisingly, a much smoother ride. Go figure. To the innocent non-majickal passerby, the road is seemingly not there. In fact, the trees and shrubbery that line each side of the road are a solid stretch. This no longer made me yelp, like when I came to my first Gathering and we drove into what I thought was a solid wall of forest. I now expected the sudden turn into the trees even though I still can't figure out how one knew where to turn. Practice, I suppose.

On we drove for a mile or so until a makeshift parking lot came into view. Here Maerik parked the car alongside a black Mercedes and killed the engine. "Have you got your crystal?" He asked, closing the car door and facing me over the hood.

"Yes, it's right here." I said, holding it up for him to inspect over the top of the car.

"Off we go then." He marched off down the beaten path.

The clearing was massive. White robed practitioners all around formed a perfect circle, talking quietly among their neighbors. Maerik took his place in the circle behind the altar as second in command. I walked to the center to join Kai and Mica.

The altar is covered in white silk, for purity, and adorned with anointed candles. At the center on the lowest tier was an athamae wrapped in yet more white silk and embroidered with ancient, ceremonial ruins stitched in gold wire, pulled thin as thread. The middle tier contained three double ringed pentacles made with strips of blue fabric. Between the outer and inner circles were ruins, again stitched in gold wire.

Kai, Mica, and myself were not permitted to talk until the ceremony required it, though we did exchange a few nervous glances. We took our spots. Spaced evenly inside a large pentacle that had been carved deeply into the earth beneath our feet, we stood there in silence.

After what seemed to be an eternity, but was all of five minutes, a bell tolled. Our heads dropped and our hands were joined with the right arm over the left. Another toll of the bell was our cue to begin the chant. With ritual verses spoken, our hands fell to our sides just as a white flash went off around the perimeter of the gathering ground. A gold, flame-like light leaped around our circle and traced the star inside. A hazy red dome appeared around the perimeter of our enclosure. The protections were raised. No one could enter or leave until the end of the ceremony.

Turning to face the altar, we saw the leaders approaching it. Victoran, the leader of our coven, said a prayer to the deities and lit some frankincense in a bowl at the top center of the altar. When Victoran finished he called us forward. "Kai, Mica, Matthias. Come forward and present your offering."

Stepping up to the altar, we each placed our crystals into

the pentacles of the Rite. Victoran unwrapped the athamae and, taking it in his left hand, struck each of the Crystals of Power. A resonating sound resulted, permeating the circle, as he called the necessary deities to bless the crystals.

Victoran read each of us a set of vows, asking if we would forsake the Dark Majicks, and those who worked them, along with other things. We all accepted, naturally. Raising the athamae in his left hand once more he brought it down three times, slicing the edges of the circles enclosing our crystals.

Another member of the coven, Centurum, third in command, strung the crystals to a leather thong. Maerik, my now former master, stepped around the altar and picked up a crystal by the thong, as did Victoran and Centurum. Each stepped before the Crystals' owners and placed them around our necks.

As soon as the crystal touched my skin it blazed white hot and threw a lingering flash of purple flame. As I saw two identical flames to either side of me, I passed out.

*   *   *

When I awoke I was no longer wearing my robes, but

instead my night clothes. Attempting to stand, I received a massive headache that was vaguely similar to the time we had decided to sample some scotch from Maerik's liquor cabinet. Yeah, that is what this feels like. Although I hadn't drank anything since Maerik had found us all passed out on my bedroom floor with an empty bottle of scotch on the desk. It was an expensive bottle of scotch too. He cuffed us upside the head and put us all to work. His study was a mess, a total pig sty.

There were foot steps in the hall just beyond my door. In walked Maerik and Mehrt, another Loedium Fertum member. He specialized in mending ailments of the body. "Ah, you're awake." Mehrt said cheerfully.

With a groan I replied, "Yes, and not so loud." I winced as another stab of pain coursed through my body and right into the back of my head. "What happened? Nothing like that has ever happened before. Go on, tell me, what was it?" Another stab of pain from the growing volume of my voice.

Mehrt looked at Maerik who nodded. "Well, there was an incident–"

"I know damn well there was an incident!" I half yelled

cutting him off and ignoring the harsh pain in my head. "It's not often that a crystal burns skin and causes one to pass out–" my rant stopped as I remembered my crystal. Where was it? It never gets removed! "What the–" I said softly, almost inaudible. "How are Mica and Kai, are they okay? Where is my Crystal of Power? You had no right to remove my Rites!"

"Mind your tongue boy!" Maerik, always on me about manners and insolence.

I opened my mouth to show Maerik just how well I could "mind my tongue" when Mehrt, sensing my outburst, cut me off. "So many questions! Well, to start with, no it is not everyday that this happens. In fact, this hasn't happened ever, so far as I can remember. Kai and Mica are no worse off than you are and are on their way here now. They recovered a bit faster than you have. As for your crystal, you still have it." He said, handing me a mirror, "And I fear we could not have removed it if we had wanted to."

Then I saw it, there are my chest, just above my heart, was a star shaped scar. Around it were flecks and stripes of scar tissue. About my neck was a band of ruins that

12

completely encompassed my neck. I reached up to touch the wounds and winced as a fiery tendril of pain coursed through me.

"What's happened to me?" I whispered. I got up to take a closer look in the larger mirror over my closet. "Can't you heal this Mehrt?"

"No." He said, plainly, catching me as my legs buckled. When had I ever been this weak? "I've tried everything I know. They seem to be coming along nicely though. A few moments ago the scars on your chest and neck were like puffy red meat. At this rate, you'll be fine in an hour or so." He lowered me onto the edge of my bed and gave me a steaming mug. "Drink, it will help with the pain."

I took a sip, scalding my tongue and numbing the pain away at the same time. It was strong, though I couldn't recognize the ingredients. "Are you going to tell me why and how this happened?" Still thinking about the contents of the mug, I blew gently over the top of the liquid inside and took another sip, letting it run down my throat and chase away the pain in my head and the rest of me.

"I think we should wait until the others arrive, don't you?

They'll want to know too, I should think, and I believe we might as well tell you all at the same time. Besides, your masters will know better than I." Turning out of the room, Mehrt added, "Now, I think they'll want some of my pain potion as well. I should prepare some more." He left.

"Maerik, will you tell me what's—"

"Not now, boy! The others will be here in a moment, have patience." He followed Mehrt.

Slowly I stood, testing my strength, then I took a step, followed by another shaky step. I finished the contents of the mug and set it on the nightstand. Shutting the door, I made my way to the wardrobe and grabbed a pair of loose, black jeans and a red T-shirt that fit snugly against my chest and back. It barely chaffed the scar on my chest, a good sign, but I just needed to feel safe, and the snug shirt helped to accomplish that.

When I'd finished dressing I picked up my now empty mug and went downstairs to the kitchen. There, rinsing it out, I poured a cup of freshly made coffee. After adding a splash of creme I made my way into the sitting room.

Mica and Kai were already there, along with Friedrik and Jonathan, their old masters. They had similar markings on their necks, but they were both wearing button-down shirts so whether or not they had a scar on their chests I couldn't tell. I suspected they did.

Sitting across from them on the leather couch I asked, "Are you guys okay?" I pulled up a coaster and sat my mug on it after another sip. Maerik went nuts when you didn't use a coaster.

"We're fine." They chorused. "Can we get down to what has happened to us?" Mica spoke up, taking the words from my mouth, thus freeing it to drink more coffee, allowing the hot liquid to warm my throat, heating me from the inside.

Friedrik began. "Well, I suppose–"

Kai interrupted, "Mattes, is that coffee?"

"Yes, help yourself, it's in the kitchen." I answered with an inward sigh. "Mica, I suppose you'll be wanting a cup as well." I nodded in the direction of Kai and the kitchen.

"Well, I guess..." he got up, reluctant.

"I should probably show them where the condiments are."

I began to feel uncomfortable with them all staring as they were. Plus, a quick chat with Mica and Kai wouldn't hurt. So I followed them out of the room into the kitchen.

On the way out someone chuckled and said: "They were so anxious to know everything, and now all they can think about is coffee." Laughing lightly, I continued to the kitchen.

"You both have ruins on your necks I see, but do have a scar on your chests as well?" I asked joining them at the kitchen island and sitting on a stool that lacked a back.

Mica spoke first, "Yeah, how'd you know?"

"I have one too." I lifted my shirt. Kai and Mica did the same.

Mica had a crescent shaped scar turned on its side, angled up, with a pointed cross through it and enclosed in a circle. Kai's was a pentagram with a ruin at its center.

"I suppose we should join the others and find out why we must be marred for the rest of our lives." Kai said, walking back to the sitting room.

When I returned to my seat across from Mica and Kai, I noticed that everyone but us three had glasses of brandy,

16

something none of us envied.

Friedrik spoke first. "What has happened to you boys hasn't happened in such a long time that we thought it a legend. You have become a triumvirate."

"Wait, I thought Maerik centered a triumvirate. How is this is a legend when it happened so recently?" Mica asked, keen to get down to it.

There was a long silence as Johnathan refilled his glass. Taking a swig and swirling the contents of the goblet he continued for Friedrik. "You three; Mattes, Kai, and Mica, he addressed us individually, are a Trincan Triumvirate." He paused for a sip of brandy and to allow us to process this. "This is the most powerful bond among majicians."

"You are descendants of the ancient Trinca ." Maerik picked up. "We thought their race and power extinct. They call their power not only from themselves or their crystals, but from the elements."

"Yes, but who is our center?" I asked.

"We're not sure, but we believe, I believe, that it is you, Mattes." Jonathan answered after a quick glance to the left and right at Friedrik and Maerik.

"But I'm no leader. I'm not even that strong!" I refused to believe that I could be the center of anything.

"Matthias, you've always been our center. You hold both of our interests, you are the mediator. You have been the keystone of our friendship for the three years that we have known you." Mica, always blunt and painfully right and sincere.

Then Kai spoke, "It's true, Mattes, Mica and I hated each other before you came along. You befriended us both and in turn we had no choice but to hang out."

"Matthias, this is something that you must accept. It's your duty and your destiny, all three of your destinies. There is no mistaking it." Victoran stepped from the shadows, I hadn't realized he was there. He was quiet. He hadn't said a thing until now, just lurked in the shadow that the secluded corner behind the couch supplied. "You took the strongest of the blow at the gathering. It took you the longest time to recover." He pulled a silver vial with engravings on it from inside his black suede trench coat. One of the engraved ruins meant sight, then it struck me, this was Guckenwasser! A rare and

18

very hard potion to make, it allowed a majician to see ties, bonds, protections, and even spirits and deities. It is powerful. "Even now I see the cords of power that link you to Kai and Mica. The majick between you is strong, when disciplined, possibly stronger than that of Maerik's, mine, and Centurum's joining."

"No, this is crazy. I can't believe this, you must have made some kind of mistake." I was on my feet, "I didn't ask for this, any of it–" Victoran held the silver vial before me.

"See for yourself," he removed the stopper and placed the open vial in my hands. Hesitantly, I placed a drop in each eye then looked at my companions before me. Strong, thick cords were there, connecting us, binding me. The cords led to me, joining us at the scars above our hearts.

"How can this be?" I whispered, backing from the room toward the hall leading to the stairs.

I think I had been in my room for an hour when Mica and Kai strode through the door. "It's true, you know." Mica said. "You were still glowing when they put you in the car. Neither of us passed out."

"Great, now you all think I'm weak or something." I groaned in complaint. "Is that why they all stare at me?"

"Matthias, they can't stop gawking at us, either! It's not just you. I can't stand it! Urgh!" Kai punched the wall in frustration.

"Hey, be careful! We just put those walls in a month ago." I rebuked.

"Ah, Mattes, you should have seen it! When the crystal touched your skin, all the protective majick flew into you. One moment the dome was there, and the next," he paused, as if lost for words. "And the next you were radiating with power. It was brilliant." Mica reminisced.

"Why don't you guys stay here tonight and in the morning we can go and pick out my car." I wanted to change the subject momentarily. "Plus, we can look up some stuff on those Trinca characters."

Mica spoke first. "I'm in, besides, we might as well find out what we can do."

I looked questioningly at Kai who pretended to think, "I don't know..." I raised an eyebrow. "Oh, what the hell. Hold on, how will we get to the car dealer?"

"Oh, Maerik is going to let me borrow his car." I answered.

"Really?" Mica and Kai asked suspiciously at the same time.

"Umm...wait here a minute." I ran down stairs. Maerik was still talking to Friedrik, Jonathan, Mehrt and Victoran. "Maerik? Can I use your car tomorrow? I want to go and see if I can find a nice set of wheels."

"Absolutely not!" He yelled, loud enough that Kai and Mica were probably laughing like crazy.

"Thanks!" I yelled, grabbing the keys off the coffee table where my rejected mug sat, now cold. "Oh, and Mica and Kai are staying the night so they can come with me in the morning." I called, retreating up the stairs. Halfway up the stairs I heard Maerik mutter "Damn kids."

Laughing, I found Kai and Mica innocently pouring over an upside down book. "What'cha readin'?" I asked, knowing they had been laughing like morons and only just managed to stop as I walked into the room.

"Oh, nothing interesting." they said together, not looking up. "You get those keys?" One of them asked with a grin that was just a touch too cheeky.

"Oh, yeah," I held up the car keys. "He was glad to help out. By the way, your book is upside down."

They looked up at me, then at each other and started to laugh again. "Glad, did you say?" Kai managed through a fit of incessant laughter.

"It sure sounded like he thought it was a good idea." Mica added, causing me to join in on the hysterical laughter.

After the laughter came to an end we each donned a book, legal pad, and pen and got to work taking notes on anything of interest. So we went on like that in silence. Until, three pots of coffee and several hours later Mica exclaimed softly, "Holy shit!"

Kai and I went over to him on the couch, "What is it?" I asked.

"Well, it says here that we can converse with our minds!" He explained, an excited tone creeping into his voice.

"What? No way!" Kai argued unconvincingly.

"Maybe we should get some rest and do some more work

when we get back tomorrow." I suggested, not wanting to venture into this subject at the moment.

"Sure, uh, do you have anything other than that pull-out-bed to sleep on? The bar in that couch-bed of yours is murder on the back." Mica complained.

"Yeah, the floor." I grinned.

I awoke the next morning around ten, which ruined my plans for an early start. Throwing off the covers I rolled out of the bed and grabbed an MSI shirt and a pair of black and red flannel patterned jeans and headed off to take a shower. When I finished and was making my way back to my room I tripped just inside the door. I went sprawling and my clothes flew out of my arms.

"Mattes! What are you doing? It's way too early, what is it, like six am?" I had woken Mica.

"It's ten fifteen in the morning, and I tripped." I retorted, nursing my foot.

"What did you trip on you club-footed klutz?" Apparently Kai had been trying to fake sleep but failed.

"I don't kno...who put these bags here?" I asked, pulling

one over, they were full of clothes. Friedrik and Jonathan hadn't forgotten Mica and Kai.

"Awesome, clothes! Friedrik does care!" Kai said, coming over and looking at the contents of the bags before taking the one belonging to him. "I could go for a shower, too."

"As could I, did Jon leave me a bag?" Mica inquired, coming over to check.

"Um, yeah, I hope you two don't plan to hop in together. My shower really isn't so large...."

"Mattes, you're incorrigible!" Mica grabbed his bag and shoved me backwards in one motion.

"Hey, I never said you couldn't." I went on, ignoring their protests. "I mean, Maerik's master bath could house you two lovers." At that I was attacked by Kai and Mica.

Finding a way out of the scuffle I told them to shower. As Kai grabbed his bag and headed off to the adjoining bathroom that connected to my room, I took a bit of chalk and a candle out of the closet where I kept all my majical paraphernalia.

Settling into my circle and focusing on the flickering candle flame, I quickly found a steady breathing rhythm and relaxed.

I let my consciousness flow down into myself to that glowing center that was my core, where all of my power rested. When had it gotten so bright, I was looking at two tendrils of power flowing from me to Mica and Kai which had not been there before. I followed one which led to Kai and thought: *Are you soon done in there? Mica wants a shower too, you'll use all the hot water!*

There was a loud thunk as, I suppose he fell, not expecting an intrusion. *Get out! You don't just barge into a guy's mind un-invited! It's indecent! You can't see what I do, can you?* I just laughed and retreated back along that connection, breaking the tie to our minds.

When I came out of my trance, Kai was standing against the wall, and Mica was in the shower. I was about to leave my circle when I saw the murderous gleam in Kai's eyes. "Hey Mattes, why not come out and play?"

"Uh, I'm fine, thanks." I didn't want to fight, and I could see that this was where that was going.

Mica came out of the shower toweling his head in a dark green band T-shirt, the band I was unfamiliar with, and blue jeans. "What's going on? Mattes, come out of there, lets go."

"I'm not coming out of nowhere unless you call off Fido over there." I pointed at Kai.

"What did you do, Mattes?" Mica wanted to know.

"Nothing!" I defended, indignant.

"He was trying to peep at my little boy bits, he was!" Kai half yelled, half whispered. "He just barged into my mind, he caused me to fall flat on my–"

"You mean we can really mind-speak?" Mica interrupted what was sure to be a long succession of curses.

"Yes." I said simply.

"That's amazing!" Mica exclaimed.

"Yeah, until you're in the shower." Kai grumbled.

"Little boy bits, did you say?" I asked, suppressing a snort of laughter and placing emphasis on "little." Hey, he walked right into that one. I was purely enjoying this advantageous opportunity.

"Argh!" He rushed me, slamming right into the invisible barrier between himself and I.

"God, Kai, I didn't see anything. Do you have something to

be ashamed of?" I was really on a roll here. "Can we just go? I won't barge into your mind while you're in ah, intimate situations, okay?" I decided to stop while I was ahead, though one more just for fun.

"You were looking!" Kai screamed, his face turned red, though I suspected not from anger.

"No, I wasn't, but thanks for letting us know what took you so long." Mica and I were both suppressing huge bursts of laughter. Kai got redder still. "Let's go." I said, rubbing out a chalk line and blowing out my candle.

I followed Mica out, wearily passing Kai. "Do we have time for a cup of coffee?" Mica asked.

"No, besides, I was planning on a Starbucks detour." I answered, opening the door that connected the downstairs hall to the garage. "Nothing like an almond biscotti and a double shot of espresso."

We sat by the window seat in the back of the shop in a nice secluded corner. I got a white chocolate, almond biscotti, drizzled with caramel and a caramel latte. Kai and Mica both got tall double mocha chips and a large brownie each. I'll never understand why they never got along before me.

"Can we really mind-speak? That wasn't some charade you two did to pull one on me, was it?"

"Hell no!" Kai said, drawing the attention of the other tables toward the front of the sitting area. He got up and walked over to another table and grabbed an ashtray. Sitting down again, he lit a Newport. "Do you think I would incriminate myself like that?" He kept his voice softer and leaned in toward us a bit, smoke rolling into my face.

"Since when do you smoke?" I managed to say through coughing and gagging.

"Since last summer, I'm nearly eighteen so get off my back, all right?" He tried to justify his disgusting habit. "I don't want Friedrik to know, he would kill me, so keep it quiet, will you?"

"Fine," I rebutted. "But keep your cancer sticks out of the car, Maerik would kill us both if he knew you were smoking in there. He has the nose of a dog, besides, the upholstery is new." I sniffed.

"So," always eager, Mica changed the subject. "How do

we talk with our minds?"

"Not sure," I tried to answer. "I just sort of figured it out. I started to meditate when I found these two strands of power leading away from my core, so I followed them. The one I followed happened to be Kai's. Then I just thought, you know. I'm not sure if it can be done outside of that state or not, possibly with practice. We should work on it, it could be useful."

"How are you paying for this car?" Kai wanted to know, clearly not comfortable with the current topic, given the events of this morning.

"Well, that corner looks promising. It works for hookers anyway." I said, voice thick with sarcasm. "With cash you dolt. I've been saving for years; birthday money, allowance, change from my spending money that Maerik would give me. I saved everything, and kept adding it to a savings account so it would collect interest. Plus, just about everything I made last summer working at Joe's Diner."

"How much do you have?" Mica inquired.

"A few grand." I mumbled over the top of my cup, feeling

as if saying the amount was too much like bragging. Kai and Mica whistled.

"So, what are you thinking of buying?" Mica went on. "And don't say 'a car,' we know that much."

"I'm not sure, a convertible would be nice. I want to give Maerik's shiny lil' thing a run for it's money. So it has to be sportier, and much more flashy than his Firebird. Would a Porsche be too much?"

"I don't think even you could afford something that flashy. Maybe a rusted, thirty-year-old one that is missing the engine. Though, it still may be a few thousand too much." Mica remarked.

"I suppose, but a guy can dream. You two ready?" I sighed, regretfully.

"Yeah." They chorused, standing.

"Kai, douse that, that nasty health risk of yours. I don't want holes in the upholstery, not to mention that nasty smell." I got into the car and buckled up.

"I don't see the big deal." Kai mumbled, stepping on his cigarette and getting into the passenger seat.

We pulled up to the dealer around midday, I parked and got out, pressing the lock button on the key pad when the other two followed suit. Halfway to the office door I remembered to arm the alarm and finished my trek to the door.

Inside I requested to see a sales representative who bustled out promptly.

He gave us the "Grand Tour," then asked what my price range was, when I told him, he whistled softly and said, "Well, I have the perfect thing for you." Walking over to a puke green monstrosity, he attempted to make it seem like the icing on a cake. "This little number just came in. She's a beauty. We just re-built the engine and put in a new transmission–"

I cut him off, not in the mood for a salesman to try and pull the wool over my eyes. "Cut the crap, will you? I'm young, but sure as hell not dumb! Show me something worth my while, I hear Sean's Chevrolet has a nice lot to pick from." Kai and Mica were covering grins with their hands. I wasn't serious, of course. I had heard bad things about the aforementioned car dealer, but he didn't need to know that.

He quickly led me over to a red Firebird, to which I quickly shot down with a forceful "no" before I was blown away by a rush of hot air. "Do you have any convertibles? A nice, un-rundown convertible from this century, something newer?" I decided to get down to the point before he had us here all day, trying to sell us a big, fat, juicy lemon. "Oh, and be careful with what you try to sell me. I'll be expecting at least a two year, ninety-thousand mile warranty, and I'll be having it checked over by my mechanic here." I nodded toward Kai. He looked a few years older than he was and he was a bit scruffy with a lightly muscled build from playing football and soccer. He looked the part. Thankfully, the sales guy didn't call my bluff.

The next car he showed me was a black convertible, the year on the window was two-thousand-four, no rust, and shiny, not a scratch. "Kai, do your thing." I wasn't sure if Kai knew exactly what his "thing" was, but he made a big show of checking wire connections, oil, and a ton of other things. All the while Mr. Sales Schmuck tugged on his too tight collar and a fine sheen of sweat coated his forehead in the sixty five degree weather.

Kai surfaced, slightly covered in oil, which was a nice

effect, and said, "Looks good." He walked around, kicking the tires to check the air pressure and pushed hard on the rear end, which sprung back up and settled promptly, which I hoped was a good sign. "Should probably take it for a test drive though, just to be sure." He added the last with a menacing look at Wonder Lungs, the car salesman.

It ran well, it was a good car actually. When I said "I'll take it" the sales representative let out an audible breath of air that he quite possibly hadn't realized he was holding. I ended up with a three year, ninety-thousand mile warranty, suck up.

I walked Kai and Mica back to Maerik's Mercedes and grabbed my half empty coffee, now cold, while Mica got into the passenger seat. When I stood up and handed Kai the keys, he was driving the car home, he asked, "You didn't really look at anything, did you? You were just screwing around, right?"

"Huh, oh, that, well you know how I like to size up the competition." I told him, keeping my face surprisingly straight and suppressing a major laugh.

"Oh, I'll get you for this." He so graciously informed me, "I don't give a damn if you were just screwing around."

I turned and began to walk toward my new car then said, "I'll have you leave my line of business out of this, so what if I favor the corner of First and Third?" Then finished walking to my car while Kai tried to figure out that what I had just said was a jest.

On the way home I contemplated my jesting at Kai and thought better of it. I decided to apologize as soon as we got home. I almost felt bad for him, I probably should have used Mica as my guinea pig anyway.

I pulled into the garage behind Mica and Kai, then headed upstairs. Halfway up the short staircase, I said to Kai, " You know I was just joking all of this morning, right? I would never intrude on you like that. I may have gone too far. But really Kai, you should know me better than that."

"Yeah, but Mattes, it wasn't fair that you put me in a situation like that." He said back to me.

"I know, and I'm sorry." I looked at his eyes, he looked a little hurt. "I was just having fun, I got carried away."

"I'm glad you were having fun." He said.

"I'm sorry, okay?" I said more firmly. "Let's just get some

coffee and study a bit."

"Fine." He said.

Attack

In the months since the fateful coven meeting which had inadvertently changed our lives, Kai, Mica, and myself began to acquire new abilities which were troublesome, at best, to understand. Our minds had been linked together so that sharing thoughts and ideas became a commonplace occurrence between us. Some found it unnerving when one of us randomly burst into laughter when the thoughts of the other amused him.

It took some time to regain control over our abilities, gone were the incantations and complex wordings for spells, and in their place was installed an ability to simply decide with which element to best carry out a task, and then to just make it happen, as though a switch could be flicked on or off allowing the power to flow from our cores. Of course our abilities weren't limitless in this manner, we could only use the elemental energy which we had amassed from our surroundings and stored within our bodies, in our cores. If needed we could draw on the elemental energy around us, or simply manipulate the energy in existence around us.

We had taken to sitting in my room reading through ancient Trinca texts and scrolls which we managed to borrow from various coven elders. It was here where we began to learn about the bulk of our abilities, and how to gain better control over the energy we possessed within our cores.

"A wise mage will have his core in order and well organized, so that his majick flows freely from its source and so that he might better understand from where his feed lines exist." I looked up from the scroll I held in my hands and looked at Kai and Mica in question, wondering if they had made any more sense of the statement than I. "What do you think?"

Mica took the scroll from me and scanned over the line I had just read. "When was the last time you guys looked at your core?"

"Well, not since we learned that we could look at that part of our metaphysical self. I kinda just took it for granted, I knew it was there, but just never really gave it much attention." Kai said. "I remember it was some giant jumbled mess though, color flashing everywhere, if color is the word for it."

"Exactly! What if we're able to organize it, you know, put it in containers or something within ourselves. Keep each element separate, maybe that's what it means." Mica said quickly. "When I try to do anything now, it just seems like I have to dig around for something, like a doctor digging for a vein. I know it's there, my majick, but I sometimes have to search to find exactly what I'm looking for. You know?"

"I have noticed that my core is constantly expanding. I generally glimpse it when I meditate." I said after a minute. "I guess it wouldn't hurt to try and separate it and understand it a little better. I have noticed the digging sensation when trying to do some of even the most basic of things as well. I suppose this could help with that."

"So why don't we try, then?" Mica said, setting the scroll on my desk and taking a seat on my floor.

Since we had began being able to cast circles with our conscious thought, we have stopped using the chalk and candle method of meditation entirely. I followed Mica to the floor and created a circle in my mind around me, reinforcing it and creating a dome of energy around me to keep my consciousness and energy from escaping my control.

I quickly arrived at the unfamiliar, jumbled mess that was my core. Colors blurred my vision. If only I could get it to stop moving, flowing, and dancing around inside me. Electrons in an electron cloud, my core was just as chaotic. I envisioned it in a bowl but that seemed to do nothing but create a basin of contorting color. I put it in a cage but the tendrils just escaped through the bars, no matter how small the gaps. In frustration, I reached out and clamped down upon the swirling mass and refused any struggle it gave.

Whenever a tendril of power escaped my metaphysical fist or gap in my concentration I poked it back in and redoubled my efforts, focusing my thoughts and concentration upon containing the power in my fist, taming it. Slowly, minutely, the power began to cease its struggle.

At long last the power stopped fighting me and yielded to

my control. In my open palm lay four perfect spheres of varying colors: red, blue, green, and yellow. And there it was, my crystal! It rested there in my core, previously hidden somehow, below the elemental majick that I thought had become my only majick.

Beginning to feel the drain of separating the majicks in my core, I began working quickly, placing each ball in its own metaphysical basin. Small tendrils of power once more began floating around in my core. I immediately thought the balls of power I had just tamed were beginning to dissolve. Checking each in turn, I noticed that they were not dissolving back into chaos, but I was absorbing new power. I connected each of these new tendrils to their basins and lead a strand of power from each basin to my crystal, hoping that would allow me to access the power more easily.

When I was entirely myself again, I allowed the barrier between myself and the rest of the world to evanescence into oblivion. My body was covered in sweat as I stood on unsteady feet and sat heavily on my bed, exhausted. "What did you guys manage to accomplish?" I asked, looking around my room for a glass of water.

"I couldn't get any of it to hold still at all, every time I tried to contain it, the majick would simply escape my control." Mica explained, clearly unsatisfied with his results.

"I pretty much had the same luck." Kai said. "What about you? Did you manage to gain some control over any of it?"

"Actually yeah, I just latched onto it and refused to let go until it bent to my will." I said. "After that I conjured some metaphorical basins in my core and placed each element in it's own basin. It seems to have worked well. There is a constant flow of energy into us, as we thought, so I just led the energy into their respective basins to keep everything going in the right place. Hopefully it worked."

"It seems like neither of us have found the right way to 'tame' our majicks," Kai made little quotation marks with his fingers when he said "tame."

Mica and Kai continued to work on controlling their elemental majicks over the next couple of days, and I poured over some of the other books we had borrowed, occasionally coming across something of interest and making a note of it across our mental link. There was so much information to absorb and for some reason I had this sensation somewhere deep within my subconscious thought that kept driving me forward, demanding myself to move faster, to get through more material, to memorize more and more and more. I kept trying to subdue it, to reason and rationalize with myself that this feeling was ridiculous, that it was simply my inquisitive nature demanding more information sooner. I wish I had listened to my subconscious, I wish I had known that time was of the essence, that life as I knew it would all too soon change irrevocably. But I didn't, destiny is a fickle friend, a fickle friend indeed.

*   *   *

It seems like only yesterday we stood in that circle at that fateful Gathering Ground and received our rites, swore oaths to uphold the values of the Majician's Code and to protect the sanctity of life from any who seek to destroy it. I had been living my semi-normal life, naïve of what really exists out there in our cruel world. Of all the realities I had to be born into, it would have to be one riddled with majick and metaphysical chaos.

Almost six months had passed since the day that changed our lives forever, setting the wheels of destiny in motion toward some grand scheme. All too soon I found myself driving down streets black with night. A new moon overhead offered no light to the thick darkness outside my car. The eerie dark whipped by the windows while Kai, Mica, and myself drove silently on toward the gathering ground. I suspect we all felt that there was something strange about this darkness, something off about it, but none of use bothered to speak. We sat in total silence, not even thoughts floating between us.

When we got to the road that was hidden by trees, shrubs and heavy brush from the road it connected to, like last month and the months before since I received my Rites, there were no trees. I slowed the car to a crawl. I knew there was some kind of enchantment or illusion on the turnoff, but I didn't expect it to go away when I received my Rites as a majician.

I took the turn, gravel crunching loudly under the tires and weaved my way around the snaking road until I arrived at what served as a parking lot to the attendants and members of Loedium Fertum. I found an empty space between two other cars, and turned the key, the engine going quiet immediately. The silence was deafening. I looked at Kai, then

Mica, and said, "Well, here we are. Guess we should go join the circle, huh?" We went and joined the circle, feeling no more at ease in doing so.

Soon the ritual versus were spoken and the barriers that kept out anything we didn't want in our circle appeared. Nothing could cross through it, and anyone with ill intentions who should touch the majical seal would befall some horrid fate. The purple, opalescent dome of power towered above, light swirling over its surface, casting the faintest purple glow on the ground where the dome of energy met with the ground. My sense of unease was still present and in no way reassured by a massive dome of energy. I must just be on edge, anxious over the previous events here. Every time I entered the circle I expected something odd to happen. This is also the first I'd seen some of these people since the night we'd received our Rites since most meetings were not mandatory. This one though, was.

We went through the usual discussions. Masters, which included Kai, Mica, and myself now, were asked if they had sensed any new majicians in our zone, discussions as to whether some of the previously sensed majicians were ready to be approached yet and brought into the coven under a master for training. This was generally done soon after their abilities hit their first peak, when they began doing majick against their own will, like when I set my birth parent's sofa on fire. Discussion continued with some of the known dark practitioners in the area and what actions should be taken.

There were cries for war or open hostility toward some of the more prominent dark groups. Others were indifferent. I didn't want a war, but I'd fight if I had to. Congress had decided it was only appropriate that we police our own, since modern jails were a bit easy for most majicians to escape. For war though, we needed a reason, and we had none good enough as of yet. Many of the zealots didn't care though, and never have, and would gladly destroy anyone who even looked like they had been using dark majick.

All the while my sense of unease was growing, I felt like I had a lump forming in my stomach. At the very edge of my peripheral vision something caught my eye, but I shoved it off as a passing light swirl on our protective circle. Then I saw it again, this time I turned my head and stared at the spot where I thought I saw something move, and projected the image of what I was seeing down our mental link to Kai and Mica. *Don't look.* I warned, not wanting whoever may be there to notice that I had actually seen them.

An arm, or what looked like an arm, cast in darkness shifted to adjust a robe, and I pointed this out over our mental link, getting confirmation from Mica that he had seen it too. I stepped forward into the center of the circle and yelled "Servo nos valde Asharah!" Another dome of light instantly went up, orange this time, over the first. From what I could tell, it looked almost solid, but it wasn't quite opaque.

I conjured light around the circle which revealed hundreds of dark robed figures emerging from the surrounding trees, forming their own circle around that of their own. Our group stayed calm, though my heart was racing like a stampede of buffalo pounding across a plain of sun-hardened dirt. Maerik, Johnathan and Friedrik were directing our coven members into positions around the circle. We were outnumbered, how many to one I'll never know. I was hoping this wouldn't come to a fight, dear God don't let this come to a fight. There can be some diplomacy between dark and white covens, right?

Wrong. A smooth, deep, mesmerizing voice made itself

heard over the small clamor in our circle. "Give us the boys and we might let you live." What boys, us? Kai, Mica, and me? A thousand thoughts were flying through my head, but the one at the very forefront was that I was going to die. I knew, somewhere deep, deep inside me, that Maerik would never willingly surrender me, or Mica and Kai for that matter. Not to something that would quite possibly end up hurting us in any way. I knew I would fight to the death to save him, too. Maerik has been the only real solid thing in my life for over three years. He was the only person who ever really loved me, like you should love your children, the only person who cared. He was harsh sometimes, he expected so much from me, greatness that I just don't believe that I'm capable of, but Maerik believed in me, really believed in me.

"Never Joshua. You dare assault us on our Sabbath? You dare return here after everything you've done, after what you've become, what you've allowed yourself to become?" Maerik clearly spoke of some past event that I was unaware of. I could tell, hear it in his voice, that he was afraid. There were so many of them, so many, and so few of us yet he would still defend us with his life if he had to.

"Maerik, my old friend, we don't want to hurt anybody, we simply want the boys. I won't harm a hair on their heads. I promise." The man named Joshua spoke again, the hypnotic rhythm mesmerizing me, luring me.

"Friends no more Joshua, you betrayed me, my coven. You betrayed your oaths. Do your worst, Joshua, but you will not have them to play with like toys." Maerik's voice was laced with power, something ancient and crazed now, that voice could send armies marching home with a whisper.

"You leave me no choice then." Joshua gave some unseen command and the dark hooded figures around our circle raised their hands to our circle of protection. They began chanting in some language I did not recognize. Their majick began to eat away at ours. I fed the circle with what energy I could spare, drawing on the earth and the wind and pouring that energy into our shield. It did nothing to slow them, their majick eating away our own the way acid eats metal. There were a few screams as several dropped to the ground, dead, our wards overwhelming them. Amidst the feeling of remorse for the loss of human life in my stomach, I couldn't help but smirk ever so slightly as I saw this. They deserved it.

As the robed figures fell replacements stepped forward to take their place. Beginning to feel drained, I had to cease my flow of energy into the wards, saving what I had left for the fight that was to follow. Moments later there was nothing left of either wards, and the black robed figures stepped freely into the circle, their numbers immense. *Burn them, do whatever it takes, just take out as many as you can!* Our mental link was open and our consciousnesses were working as one. I felt bile forming in my throat as a ball of fire appeared in my hand and began pelting toward the nearest hooded figure's chest, too fast and unexpected for him to move. His scream was shrill and gut-ripping. I've taken a life, I thought, over and over and over again. Kai screamed in my head to pull myself together, because if we didn't kill them, they would kill us.

Collecting myself, I took in everything around me: black robes bearing down on the three of us, white robes dropping like flies, Maerik fending off a small group of his own, and other coven members in similar situations. We were on our own here, there were just too damn many of them, and no where near enough of us. Funny, how the bad guys always outnumber the good. Why does it always have to work that way?

I stopped thinking then and started reacting, blasting my way through hordes of black robes, my gut clenching involuntarily as each one burst into a pillar of flame. The stench of burning flesh left behind from the smoldering piles of ashes littered on the ground burned my nose. Thirteen, fourteen, twenty, how many more times do I have to kill today? How many more? *Mattes!* Mica was screaming in my head. I turned to face where I instinctively knew he was, shooting as many balls of fire behind me as I could muster. I began running to Mica, who was encircled by a group of dark robed figures who were very close to subduing him. I grabbed the first one I could reach with a charged hand. I don't know how or what I was doing, but when I touched him he flew across the clearing and smashed into a tree. His head slammed against the hard trunk and cracked audibly over the noise, into shards, blood and other less pleasant things falling to the ground. Disgusted with the scene, I grabbed two more, one in each hand and pulsed fire energy through my arms, down into my hands as they began to incinerate in my grasp,

51

their squeals of pain haunting my thoughts. Mica was casting off balls of fire as fast as he could at anything wearing a black robe, but he was quickly becoming overwhelmed.

I reached out with my majick, down into the Earth, calling on the wind. I raised a score of stones of varying size. "Duck!" I screamed in a voice that emanated power that I didn't know I had. Mica fell to the ground, flattening himself just as I shoved the rocks, stones and pebbles as hard as I could at the dark majicians encircling the two of us. The rocks shot through the figures, thudding as they hit, penetrated through flesh and made sucking noises on their way out. They didn't stop, the projectiles kept going, clearing a small path through the sea of black, through which I quickly saw Maerik loosing his battle. I saw Kai rushing to his aid and, screaming, I ran as fast as I could, shooting fire and stone. I summoned gales of wind, blowing the black robed figures back, but there were more and more. As I came up by Maerik's side, Mica just behind me with Kai arriving at almost the same time as I, Joshua appeared in front of Maerik. When I was less than ten paces away from my teacher, the only man who I would ever want to call Dad, my hero in many aspects, Joshua's hand moved faster than the eye could see. A black handled athamae decorated with intricate gold weaving appeared in Maerik's chest and he fell.

I ran those last ten paces in two giant strides and caught him before he hit the ground, tears streaking down my cheeks, my body racked with immediate grief. "Mattes, go, begone from this place, the three of you need to leave, now!" Maerik's voice was hoarse with inevitable death, the Dark Lady knocking at his door. A tear rolled down my cheek and dripped onto his chest as his last breath left his lips.

"You son of a bitch. You son of a bitch." I said, slowly, calmly, that unknown power emanating from my voice again. I grabbed the athamae from Maerik's chest and stood, slowly, turning. "You son of a bitch, you're going to pay for that." My voice, of no making of my own, stayed even, calm, powerful.

"Mattes, don't you see, you can stop all of this." Joshua's voice said, taking on that melodic quality once more, but my anger and grief culled any effect it had on me. "All you have to do is come with me, give yourself to the darkness and no one else has to die this night."

All I could think to say was "You son of a bitch"' So I said it. Then, "You think I would come with you? Reward you for your deeds here this night? Give up what Maerik gave to save us from your fate?" I heard several robes brushing together, the fabric making the familiar swooshing sound, somewhere close behind me, coming closer. "You've thought wrong, Joshua." I spat his name out like a curse, like it was a bad taste in my mouth that wouldn't go away. All at once, I shot a volley of flame behind me, charging the athamae I still held in my hand with all the energy I could muster before throwing it right at Joshua, the part where it flies through the air absent as it appeared instantly in his chest. "I told you, didn't I, that you would pay for your deeds tonight, and now you will answer to the Dark Lady." I stared into his eyes as he took his last breath, not caring that it made me sick to my stomach to know that I had taken yet another life, even if it was scum.

Still there were more, and the death of their marshal didn't cease their attack. Clearly, Joshua was only here to oversee that everything went smoothly this evening. There was obviously someone else who wanted us, who wanted to turn us into the dark convert that Joshua had become. I sent a thought over our mental link telling Mica and Kai to come close to me and when they were near I grabbed their hands and started chanting a spell of warding I had read in one of the borrowed books back at the house. An emerald dome of light shot up around us, soon followed by a black dome, which was not my work but was clearly crafted as a prison. As soon as our energy was depleted, we would be trapped with no escape. I thought, and I thought hard, harder than I've ever thought before, trying to think of some way to escape. "What about some sort of de-summoning spell?" Mica asked. "Word it differently, using light and air, and it just might work." Having no ideas of my own I grasped their hands tighter, not wanting them to be left behind, and pictured my bedroom, focusing until I had every detail inked into my conscious thought.

"Per filiolus, permoveo nos!" I screamed, channeling every ounce of light and wind majick still in my reserves into the spell. Nothing happened right away, though I felt my energy levels dropping quickly, and all of a sudden everything went black.

Another Time

I fought my way through the darkness for what felt like eternity; the sense of loneliness was utterly profound, having absolutely no contact with Mica or Kai over our mental link. Even when we were blocking each other, I could feel their presence, I knew they were there even if we were in different parts of a city entirely. Were they dead? Was I dead? Is this what death is like? The questions flew through my head, punctuated with Maerik falling, me catching him, the athamae appearing out of his chest. I could somehow sense that I was still alive, but I couldn't feel any part of my body, couldn't make my eyes open, couldn't move.

I lay in my prison of dark nothingness plagued with

nightmares for what felt like one lifetime after another, forced only to reflect on the worst moments of my life. No sense of the passing of time, nothing to judge how much longer I needed to exist like this.

Finally, at long last, the darkness turned murky, less opaque, then dark gray like storm clouds floating in my vision. Lighter, lighter, less and less opaque. My body began to feel like a dead weight, immobile but there. Actions like moving a finger left me feeling drained so I lay there, motionless, recharging. After some time like this, I began delving into my core to see the basins of power stored there almost completely depleted: the cords binding us together were weak and frail threads. I reached out from my core to nature, asking the wind, the earth, the pools of water underneath it and deeper even to the molten core of the land to lend me it's strength, to fill me up, to make me whole again.

Nature allowed me to draw power from it and the basins I created began to fill once more. I channeled some of this energy down our link, filling up Kai and Mica too. As time passed (Was it seconds? Hours? Days? Years? I don't know), the threads became strong cords again and my stores of power were full to almost overflowing once more. So I slept, not the bleak, never ending darkness of before, but a sleep plagued with nightmares. I relived the battle in the clearing over and over again, relived it a thousand times. I held Maerik's dying body in my arms and slew Joshua in a painful, endless cycle. When I finally woke from my slumber wrought with nightmares, my pillow and bed were soaked through with tears and sweat. Lingering tears were still streaming down my face. I wanted to throw off the covers but somehow I realized I was completely naked underneath, so I let them lay there, and tried to figure out a way to stem the torrents of tears coming down my face.

Eventually I felt drained and dried up, I felt as though there was nothing left in this world or any other worth crying for. Looking to either side of me I saw two beds, each containing it's own human lump in the center. I could make out the faces of Kai and Mica on either bed and was relived to see them here. I wasn't alone at least.

I reached out to them across our link, touching their consciousnesses. *Hey you guys, can you hear me?*

I felt something stir on the other side of the link. *Yeah, I think.* Kai said.

I'm alive? Was Mica's reply.

Can you guys move? I wondered across the link. I saw them both begin to move different parts of their body, finally stretching out and eventually coming to a similar realization that I had.

"Where in the hell are my clothes?" Mica asked.

"Same here, I'm all naked and stuff." I said.

There were voices outside the room, barely audible, but present. I could just barely make out what they were saying. "I know I heard voices, Papa." It sounded like a girl.

"Are you sure, Mel?" A man's voice.

"Yes, I'm positive." That girls voice again.

The handle creaked on the door across from us and in stepped an older man in his late thirties or early forties. His hair and goatee were fading shades of black and gray. You could make out where it had began to recede slightly where the hairline met his forehead. The wall sconce was burning long tapir candles which set his face in partial shadow. He moved across the room to our bedside. "You're awake, young mages. How do you feel?"

Like I was stepped on by a fifty ton elephant, I wanted to say but I bit back my comment and instead told him, "Okay, I think. I'm alive." My voice choked and a ball formed in my throat with the last word as my thoughts traveled back to the clearing. I saw the faces of those who fell, those who never made it out of that clearing. We were lucky, very, very lucky, to be alive.

The man stared at me with these deep, penetrating eyes that seemed to pierce down to my very core. "Good, good," he said softly. "My daughter, Melody, will fetch you boys some clean clothes. I'll ask you to join me and my family for dinner, I shall not take no for answer." He turned and followed Melody out the door, closing it gently behind him. Moments later there was a light tap on the door and Melody came bustling through, her gentle lips turned up into a smile.

She looked at me, bent her knees in the slightest curtsy, and placed a pile of clothes at the foot of my bed before retreating out the door again. I couldn't seem to form the words thank you while she was going about setting down the clothes. Though, after she left, I realized that all the clothes were at the bottom of my bed while my two companions were in separate beds five feet to either side of me. I couldn't help but laugh good heartedly at the situation.

"What's so funny, Chuckles?" Kai asked, confused.

"Well," I said. "It seems that I have a stack of clothes at the foot of my bed and the two of you are on opposite sides of me."

Realization struck not long after as Mica said, "Mattes, just get dressed under the covers and bring us some damn clothes, stop trying to creep Kai out."

"Oh, all right." I scooted down the bed, pulling the sheets with me around my waist. I pulled on what looked like a pair of white silk breeches and pair of black velvet pants and slipped them under the covers. Once I had covered the bits that would 'creep Kai out', I threw them each a similar outfit. One with maroon pants and black shirt, the other with deep, forest green pants and a pale green shirt. I slipped on my own wine red shirt while they tugged and pulled at their own clothing.

Just as we were finishing dressing there was another tap on the door and a younger looking man popped through, "Hello." He said, bowing slightly. "Pleasure to meet you, my name is Jeoffry. If you're all set, I would be glad to escort you to the dining room?"

"Of course." I said. "I'm Mattes, this is Mica, and this here is Kai." I pointed my two friends out respectively and they raised their hands in a slight wave in acknowledgment . We followed Jeoffry down a hall lit with sconces burning oil, which cast an eerie orange glow on everything and made the hall itself look grander and more majestic. We went through several halls and down one flight of stairs before arriving at a set of arched double doors that appeared to open as Jeoffry approached and went through. *Did those doors just open by themselves?* I asked Kai and Mica silently.

They probably have someone on the other side. Mica said rationally. Only as we went through and the doors closed again no one was holding them.

Really? I asked. *Maybe he's a majician too?*

Could be, that would be the simplest answer.

"Please, have a seat." The man said. "My name is Ephraim, by the way." Kai, Mica and I went through the same introductions as we had with Jeoffry and took seats at the small, mahogany banquet table. "This is my daughter, Melody, and my son Jeoffry, both whose acquaintances you have made, albeit briefly so. My younger son, Thom, isn't with us this evening."

"We're pleased to meet all of you and we're thankful for your abundant hospitality." I told him. "Would you mind, sir, telling us the name of this peculiar place?"

"Please, call me Ephraim, and this place is Käturnen, however you're in Fief Michval, and I am the Lord of this estate. Now, you three must be famished, you were out for nearly two weeks. Please, reserve your questions for the end of the meal and I'll be happy to answer them. For now, I believe it pertinent that we enjoy the lovely meal Melody and a few of our cooks have prepared for us." With that six men and women came out of the door behind Ephraim and began setting down troughs of food including a warm potato salad, a piping hot roast, a small swine with a granny smith apple protruding from its little mouth, bowls of fresh greens, a pitcher of dressing, and other things that looked absolutely delicious with names I do not know.

The three of us gorged ourselves to contentment while Ephraim and his family enjoyed modest portions of their own. At long last we ate the last bite from our plates and lay down our flatware, stuffed and content. "Now, boys, if you'll join me in the study, I'll be happy to answer any of your questions. I'm sure we have a few of our own, as well." Ephraim looked at Jeoffry as he said the last part.

Ephraim stood, and we followed him out the high double doors, down another hall, and into a small, homely room furnished with plush chairs and couches. Ancient looking pictures decorated the wall, a few of which I even recognized from trips to the museums. *Guys, this is very weird. I don't think we're even in our own time let alone country anymore.* I broadcast down our link.

What makes you think that? Kai asked.

Because the Mona Lisa is hanging on the far wall. I showed them both a picture of where I was looking.

God Mattes, you're right! Mica said, a slightly worried tone creeping over his mental voice.

"Ephraim, that is a beautiful painting over there." I pointed at the portrait of the Mona Lisa hanging over the fireplace on the far wall.

"Ah, very much so, an old friend made it as a gift for my late wife for our wedding day." His face was picturesque of a sad man as he explained the origin of the painting.

"One day that painting will sit in a building for millions to see and admire it's beauty and wonder at its origin." I said kindly.

We talked at length about the country and the fief until finally Ephraim got to what he had really been waiting to ask. "My healers tell me of marks on your neck, chest, and back, would you mind telling me how you acquired them?"

"I don't see how that's relevant to our presence here." I said, not sure if I should explain the circumstances surrounding the marks of our triumvirate of power.

"Oh it is, very much so indeed. You see, I believe you are not from around here, that much is obvious, at least. But even further I believe you existed in some other time and somehow managed to find yourself here. Am I right in assuming so?" Ephraim stared at me with his penetrating gaze, it was hard to meet those eyes but I did, and I swallowed hard, trying not to drown in their endless depth.

"I-I think so. I believe we are in another time. When I said that painting over there, the one above the fireplace, would one day be admired by the world, I wasn't lying, and it was not flattery. Where we're from that is the most famous painting in the world, it sparks mystery. Authors have written books about it and speculation runs wild about the subject and the genius who painted it." I told him.

"Interesting." Ephraim mumbled softly. "Very interesting. One day you will have to tell me more of it. It would seem then that you have indeed managed to go back in time. But why? To what end did you come here, to this precise moment in time?"

"We don't know, we were just trying to get away," Mica said softly.

"From what?" Ephraim asked, a hint of compassion in his voice.

"A band of dark majicians, they called themselves the Dark Grail." I told him. I looked at Kai and Mica and held back the sobs as I remembered Maerik's death in my arms. "They ambushed us, destroyed our coven, and killed our masters. Killed Maerik." I choked as I said his name; a single tear slid slowly down my cheek..

There was nothing but silence as I sat there, remembering the events that led up to our presence in this unknown place and time. Ephraim looked to be deep in thought, pondering something until he finally stood and started pacing the small room. The silence in the room was deafening and thick, nothing but the occasional brush of clothing broke it. Finally Ephraim spoke, "Matthias, we have a lot in common, and not just your friends and myself, but the three of you and my family." He paused, taking a breath. "You see, not only this painting on the wall here has survived the ages into your time, but also something else, something much more sinister and evil. The Dark Grail exists in this time, too. Do you understand what this could mean?"

I thought about it for some time but it was Mica who answered him. "We came, or we were sent, here, by whichever means it does not matter, to somehow prevent the slaughter at our coven meeting from ever happening."

"Of course!" I said. "I should have thought of that."

"It's only a theory, mind you, I could be wrong, but if you were to destroy the Dark Grail in this time, then there would be no Dark Grail to destroy your coven in your time." Ephraim explained.

"Ephraim, you said we had something in common, what exactly was that and what does it have to do with us?" Kai wondered aloud. I was strangely curious about that as well. He had gone directly from talking about how we had something in common and then simply skipped over it.

A look of utter remorse and longing came over both Ephraim and Jeoffry's faces. They were silent for a long time, mourning for something long gone. "It's too late for my mother, Kai, for you have only traveled back thus far. However, we can still save your masters and your coven." Now Jeoffry choked up slightly. "I inherited my majick from my mother. She was one of the King's, my uncle, mages in his personal guard..."

"The Dark Grail had her assassinated four years ago." Ephraim finished for Jeoffry where he had trailed off, suppressing ill-begotten memories and emotions. "She fought with her entire soul when they came. She fought hard and took many of them into the afterlife with her when she fell, but still she fell."

"By defeating the Dark Grail in this time, you would be saving your friends in your time and avenging my wife. I would be eternally indebted to you. But of course, I cannot ask this of you, I cannot ask you to give your lives to our selfish grief." Ephraim continued quietly, his voice barely a whisper. He was speaking as if all this were only a passing thought, to be replaced by the next. "Of course, if you were to do this I would give you whatever supplies you needed."

"Ephraim, I-I don't know. I can't answer that right now, we need to discuss it first." I told him. "And besides, what if by destroying this coven now we destroy the future we once knew?"

"This is not an easy decision to make, nonetheless one to be made lightly." He replied. "I think that shall be all for the night. We are going nowhere and you boys need your rest.

Any questions you may have can wait until tomorrow."

"I'll show you to your rooms. Since we don't really use the third floor that much you've pretty much got it to yourselves." Jeoffry stepped forward and led us out the door, down the hall, into this giant chamber with a mosaic domed ceiling, lustrous marble floors, and stairs adorned with gilt railing leading up several floors in a wide spiral. While the staircase was long, the grade was fairly modest, so climbing up was fairly easy.

The floor on the third level corridor was of a blood red marble, shot with golden veins. Floors should not be so breath-taking, I thought. There were several suites spaced along the hall and each had it's own hand carved door and elegant knob. I pushed open a door that had some runes engraved on the border and a serpentine dragon carved out of the heavy teak. I entered into a small room fit with a few chairs similar to those in the study. They were upholstered with some kind of strange burgundy velvet-like material that seemed to be more fluid than solid fabric.

Down a short hall were doors to two more rooms. One had a large gilt tub and a box with a lid covering a hole which I assumed was the toilet. We just had to travel into a time without indoor plumbing. The other room was larger, more circular, with a spectacular view of the countryside out of enormous bay windows which were draped in pale cream silk. There was a four poster bed against the wall adjacent to the door, the window on the wall adjacent to the bed. Off to the right of the door was a small walk-in wardrobe and on the other wall, across from the bed, was another smaller room with a now familiar box-thing in it. A low desk with a mirror was mounted on the wall above it and a too-small stool was positioned under the desk. A makeup room, I surmised.

There was a small library off of the main room lined with a few book shelves that were sparsely filled. Most had titles I couldn't read or didn't recognize. I made a mental note to at least look over some of them before we left here. I headed back into the main room, down the hall, and into the bedroom where I laid down and fell immediately to sleep.

I dreamed of men in dark robes moving about in a building somewhere that I didn't recognize and mumbling to each other about things I didn't understand. I was only able to catch a word or two here and there and what I did hear sounded foreign and barbaric, garbled up so as not to be understood, I supposed. I couldn't help but wonder what they were talking about as I strained to hear their words. It sounded nothing like any language I'd ever heard before.

I woke, startled, to a loud rapping on the door of the suite. "Mattes! Mattes! Come on, wake up, there's breakfast downstairs." I heard Mica's voice calling from the other side. I crawled out of bed and stumbled around until I found the shutters on the window, guided by the thin creak of light protruding through the crack between the two panels. I was blinded by the initial blaze of the sun pouring through the window and covering the room in it's liquid gold glow. I could tell by some instinct that this window faced east and the sun was just above the horizon, level with the window. It was way too early for me to be awake, let alone eat breakfast.

After my eyes adjusted a bit I noticed a pile of robes at the foot of my bed on a trunk that sat there. I put them on, leaving my old ones in a basket by the door on the way downstairs. The basket hadn't been there last night. The air inside was cool on my face, causing the last dregs of sleep to melt away halfway down the long spiral stair. Shafts of the early morning light came down from hidden windows in the domed ceiling above, giving off the illusion that the light was coming through the mosaic.

I took a seat between Kai and Mica, across from Jeoffry. Ephraim sat at the head of the table which was adorned not with platters of food. but empty plates and a small array of silverware. Half of an orange sat in a bowl on the base plate before each setting. "'Morning." I said lamely, picking up what I recognized as a grapefruit spoon and scooping out a bite of the orange. As soon as it hit my tongue my eyes nearly popped out of their sockets. The orange, or whatever it was, was the best tasting thing to ever have graced my taste buds. So sweet and tropical but not overwhelmingly so. There was a perfect balance of sweetness mixed with the slight tang of citrus and this hint of something more exotic, a flavor that I recognized but couldn't quite place. I immediately took another bite and far too soon I was staring at the hollow husk.

"What the hell was that?" I asked, surprised.

"Don't you like it?" Ephraim asked, probably amused with me having finished the whole thing in mere moments.

"The contrary, it was exquisite! An orange? No...

something sweeter, more tropical." I said.

"A variety of orange, yes. We have many here but these are by far the best. We grow them out back, my Mona planted the tree just before Jeoffry, our eldest, was born," he said, a glint in his eye as his mind wandered back to that moment. During his flash back a few of his servants collected the fruit bowls and laid down a new plate. This one was a biscuit topped with a poached quail egg and some fried ham. It was garnished with a white wine sauce and a sprig of mint. I completely devoured the delicious offering, though more slowly and with better table etiquette than the orange.

I noticed a younger boy at the table by Jeoffry while I was eating whom I supposed was the youngest son, Thom. He was perhaps a year or two younger than his brother, with short cropped sandy blond hair that laid flat over his head. "I'm Mattes." I nodded at him between bites. "This is Kai and Mica." I tilted my head in their directions and ate another bite.

"Aye mate, Thom," He nodded in turn, then said something that completely baffled me. "So, this is the Chosen?" He said it more to his father than me, and received a very stern "I'll kill you later" look in return.

"The what?" I asked.

"You know, the Chosen, 'Power of three, marks mote it be.'" Thom replied. Ephraim was politely glaring at Thom the way parents do when they want you to shut the hell up. He was completely oblivious to the very obvious daggers shooting out of his father's eyes, or he just didn't care. Rich boy syndrome? Ephraim didn't seem to be the type to spoil his kids rotten, but then again, I'd only known him for a mere moment in time.

"Thom, come now, let these boys enjoy their breakfasts," Ephraim said nonchalantly.

"You didn't tell them, did you? The three most important people in all of Käturnen, and you didn't tell them?" Thom said in a soft voice.

"Wait!" I said too loudly, "Tell us what?"

"Thom," Ephraim said. "I did not want to influence the decision they must make regarding the Dark Grail and you know that."

"Influence them? If they don't our country becomes overrun with evil mages who do nothing but pillage, torture, murder and sacrifice to the demons they call gods," Thom said, clearly upset.

"Thom, that may be true but they still have free will. They did not ask for this fate," Ephraim looked at Thom, a calm expression on his face. Thom just sat there and stared back at him.

"Would someone please tell us what is going on?" I asked, a little louder than I intended, as I became more and more frustrated.

Silence fell over the room and tainted the taste of the meal. Thom was staring down his father and his father was looking at me as though he were an appraiser and I was the priceless gem some billionaire wanted to have insured.

"During the days of the Grail's forming, some two hundred years or so ago, Cian, an Elder mage, returned after having not been seen or heard in more than five years." Jeoffry spoke as he stepped out of the corner cast in shadow. "He spoke of dark times to come; atrocious crimes, brothers killing brothers in the name of dark kings, and ancient powers awakening." He paused, letting the full weight of the words sink in. "Only three boys bearing the marks of the Elder, bound together in sacred ceremony, can drive the evil from this land."

Our triumvirate of power must be this bond, and well, the marks don't need an explanation. I could hear Mica's thought but I couldn't fathom being able to rid a world of evil. "We are just three kids, Jeoffry. In our time we've only had these marks for a few months. I don't see how we could possibly destroy something that was more powerful than our entire coven..."

"If you decide to take up this quest, you will not be alone. I will accompany you and fight along side you, for my mother." Jeoffry said.

"Jeoffry, we're four then, four against hundreds, maybe thousands. The chances of success are practically non-existent!" Mica exclaimed, discouraged by the obvious numbers.

"You three don't know what you are truly capable of, do you? You're Trinca, the Elder race, the oldest and most powerful majick to have ever existed. You've traveled centuries through time. That's no easy task." Jeoffry spoke with this voice that was touched with a passionate tone. "No, this will not be easy, and yes we very well could fail, but why should that stop the attempt? Is it worth the price? The lives of the people you loved? If you stop them here, in this time, there is no Grail in your time to destroy your coven. No Grail to terrorize the people of this time, to murder women, children, sons, brothers, and fathers. Tell me, then, is the price we pay for doing nothing worth not taking a risk?"

He's right, I conceded mentally to Mica and Kai. "No," I said, hanging my head slightly, disappointed in my selfishness.

"Where do we start?" Kai asked.

"With Cian, I should think, we need to hear his full prophecy," Mica answered the question before Jeoffry had the chance to speak.

"Why? How do you know he is even alive?" Was Ephraim's query.

"Because we need to hear that prophecy in full, there may be more to it than the abridged version passed down over centuries. I have a feeling he is alive, Cian means 'Ancient' in Gaelic and historically prophets live until the prophecy is fulfilled," Mica answered him.

"Then you start at Fief Bläd in Schötre, a small city that in ancient times was the home of the Trincan Elder race," Ephraim said. "It's settled then, you'll leave in two day's time at dawn. You'll venture to Schötre, try to learn of Cian and hopefully find him and learn what you can of the prophecy."

"Right," I said. "I think for now a very warm bath would be amiable and then if Jeoffry might be so kind as to further enlighten us on exactly what we are capable of."

"That is fair. I'll take you to the bathhouse where you can soak and bathe in the hot springs," Jeoffry told me.

We finished breakfast in moderate silence though Thom was occasionally sending harsh looks at his father. When he wasn't glaring at Ephraim, Thom was appraising us. He had a piercing stare that made my skin bump and the hair on my neck stir.

After breakfast Jeoffry took us through the labyrinthine halls and quickly explained the layout of them. They were actually fairly simple to understand and much less labyrinthine after that. The house was broken up into a few wings. One contained the kitchen and dining areas as well as all the other preparation areas, like the ovens, this wing also contained all the servant quarters and the sick rooms, like the one we were in. Another was two stories and made up the main part of the house and consisted of all the living areas for guests and entertaining, studies, and suites on the second floor. There was a third wing set aside for the family, all of their sleeping areas and private studies lay there.

We soon arrived at the front gate of the estate and continued down a quaint cobbled street with small shops and homes on either side. The roofs were flat at the center and pitched on the edges with terracotta shingles. Most rooftops had lush green plants growing and some had bridges connecting them.

The bath house was a giant building in the middle of the street which split around the building. We entered through a small arch at the front of the building, at least what looked like the front to us, which was immediately across from the split in the road around this massive building. It sat within its own little oasis of lush greenery and fountains fed presumably by the pressure created from the hot water of the springs through underground pipes. A tranquil layer of steam nestled over the water, swirling with the gentle breeze. A stone path, built just above the water, began at the point of the road and split in three different directions. The left and right paths lead toward two little sitting areas which were shaded by beautiful broad leaved trees and exotic flowers doting the plump bed of grass. No one occupied the area and it looked undisturbed. I could almost sense that no one ever went there. It was too beautiful, too perfect, to disturb.

We took the center path, which slithered through the water and into the front of the building before merging cleanly with the floor of the bath house. The walls were dimly lit and cast eerie shadows which danced along the wall as we moved through the halls. We had been greeted at the door by a younger kid, maybe thirteen or so. He led us to a door which opened to reveal a smaller chamber. Inside was a bed of steaming water about one third the size of a standard pool. The water was just a few inches below a path skirting the pool. The path was a bit larger toward the door with a stone bench carved from the wall and floor around the wall. A basket stood in the center of the room.

"You've got to be kidding," I said. "We're to bathe here? Together?"

"These springs have healing properties, can't you feel it? You're Trinca, Elder." Jeoffry said. "You can draw elemental energy from these pools to restore your body and your energy for the journey to come."

"Have something to hide, Mattes?" Kai jived.

"Hell no," I said. "Just wouldn't want to hurt your psyche and give you some sort of male ego inferiority complex."

Jeoffry was already beginning to strip down to his birthday suit but I swear I heard him say something about boats and the motion of the ocean, which made me laugh. "No one ever got to England on a rowboat, Jeoffry," Kai and Mica cracked up at the puzzled look on Jeoffry's face.

"England?" Jeoffry said, confused.

"In our time, we lived across a massive ocean from a country called England. You need a boat large enough to stand up to the huge swells the open ocean throws at you," I explained. "So a popular retort to the whole 'It's not the size of the boat, but the motion of the ocean' was 'Yeah, but nobody ever got to England on a rowboat.' It's a metaphor."

Jeoffry continued to look puzzled as he took off his last stitch of clothing, tossed it into the basket with the rest, and slid into the water with an audible sigh. We followed suit, all doing our best to avert our eyes in our boyish self-consciousness. I always found it awkward when the guys in the locker room after gym class would run around stark naked. They would have face-to-face conversations with each other and slap each other on the butt. I always made great jokes at their expense to my friends.

The three of us slipped into the water together, each a respectable distance from the other. Immediately, I felt the heat and the energy working. I sighed as inch by inch the water touched my skin and the tightness in my muscles instantly relaxed away. I could feel all sorts of elemental energy in the pool. I opened myself up to it and let it enter my core, feeling more and more alive and revitalized each second. I sat there on the bench just below the water and drank in the power, letting it heal my mind and body. "I feel like I could move a mountain," I said aloud to no one in particular.

84

"You need to close yourself off to the flow now," I could hear Jeoffry's voice, but the power felt so good, I wanted to embrace it and drink in more and more. "Matthias, the power will destroy you if you don't stop. You can only retain so much raw energy for so long."

"Mattes, come on," Mica and Kai said softly. *Come back to us, mate.* I felt mica enter my consciousness, guiding me, helping me to remember how to stem the flow of the energy and became aware of myself again. My energy reserves were full to the brim. The brightness of them was blinding, molten pieces of pure energy. I really could move a mountain...probably.

"Thanks," I said to all of them.

"Don't mention it," Jeoffry said. Then he laughed, "By the way, you all have dirty minds in your time."

I guessed he finally understood the metaphor from earlier and laughed. "Why don't you tell us of yourself? It would seem we've been going on about ourselves now for ages and you have told us nothing of you. Do you have a girlfriend? Wife? Kids?"

"Kids? Mattes, he's, like, barely twenty!" Mica said.

"I've seen those thirteen-year-old dads on Jerry Springer. Shit happens when you party naked," I said back.

"I'm well within my right to take a wife and to bear an heir but I'm not certain that I've found what I'm looking for," Jeoffry answered.

"Often we don't know what we are looking for, or we do and we're afraid of it," Mica said in a moment of wisdom that often plagues his voice.

"You're too wise, Mica," Jeoffry mused, looking at Mica with an appraising look. He dunked his head under the water and came up, spitting water and shaking his head, splashing us slightly. "Sorry."

He grabbed a small corked glass bottle from the several that sat in small groups around the pool and lathered a lavender scented shampoo through his hair and dunked his head again, rinsing, and we followed suit.

When we left the pool warm towels awaited us on the bench and we toweled off and put on the white silk shirt and underwear and black velvet breeches and left the way we came in. Jeoffry tipped the boy who led us to the pool with a few pieces of metal that glinted gold and silver and we were off. We went through the arch and over the stone path, and back down the street retracing our steps. Hours had passed, as the sun was beginning to slouch from the afternoon sky. Time seemed to speed up while we were in the pool.

Preparation

At the house Jeoffry took us to a small room with a round table at its center and leather chairs around it. A large map was drawn into the table, Käturnen written in scrolling calligraphy over a star marking the capital. We sat and listened as Jeoffry explained this country and how it was organized, as well as it's history.

Käturnen is comprised of seven fiefdoms and the capital estate where the king and queen have ruled since the evanescence of the Trinca and Elder Council who ruled the land before that. During the times of the Trinca, there were eight tribes and the Elder Council sat further north in Drät. Since the Trincan Elder disappeared and the Trincan race died off, Drät had began to go rogue. The land rejected the new leadership of the king and queen, even after the king and queen were put on their throne with the blessing of the three remaining Elders of the Last Council.

So the throne was moved to where it stands today, and Drät has become lost to the kingdom, completely defected. It was around the time of the Trincan fall that the Dark Grail began to form and take refuge in Drät where they hid for centuries, unreachable, until Marqus brought the Dark Grail from hiding. He's been terrorizing Käturnen for centuries, trying to dissolve the throne and bring back a sadistic, evil version of the Elder Council with him at it's head.

Marqus believes that Drät can be united with the new kingdom and hopes to use the power there to control it. Marqus is not Trincan nor Elder and does not have the right to use the power of the land, he controls it through dark spirits and evils of the other plane.

"We're supposedly Trincan, Elder at that. Shouldn't we be able to tame the land and force out Marqus?" I asked, hopeful.

"Drät has been poisoned by the centuries of darkness, the ancient powers are still there, but they've been tainted and suppressed by Marqus' evil majick. " Jeoffry said. "There may still be ways for Drät to be saved, but first, Marqus must be destroyed."

"Well then, it would seem then that in order to learn how to defeat Marqus and save Drät, we need to seek out Cian and learn of the prophecy and anything else he knows that could help." I said.

"I agree, but the trek to Schötre is long, neigh on two weeks, after we have learned what we can, assuming we find Cian, we can go East through a mostly forgotten mountain pass into Drät."

"How exactly do we go about finding Cian?" Mica wondered.

"Assuming he is still in Schötre, Cian will sense your presence when we get there and will hopefully find us." Jeoffry answered. "He may have already noticed your presence in this land and is simply waiting for you."

I stood and stretched my arms and arched my back, standing up on my toes, yawning. "It must be late, we've been in here for hours."

"Why don't we all get some rest and finish getting ready to set out tomorrow?" Kai suggested, and we all nodded assent and exchanged good nights with Jeoffry and left him at the table, staring at the map. We found our way to the foyer and up the stair to our rooms, where I lay on top of the sheets, exhausted, but unable to find sleep.

When sleep finally came, so did the nightmares of my departed master's death. It seems that each time the nightmare repeats, something is changed, sometimes Maerik would live, a cruel joke for when I awoke to a world where he is still dead. This time though, a tree stood in the center of the clearing, looking ancient and powerful, its bows laden with wisps of glowing mist.

For a moment I forgot the nightmare I was in and walked toward the tree that seemed to be calling to me. I was drawn to it, awed by the feeling of ancientness and majestic power radiating from the tree. I felt a presence at the edge of my mind, asking permission to enter. I knew before I even granted it that this being at the gate of my conscious mind did not need my permission, but wished only to save me from having to break my mind to enter.

To find me means to find an end
return my stolen gift
and end this blight on spirit and Earth

I heard the words echoed into my consciousness, engraved into my brain, and then the tree was gone and I was awake in my bed, birds trilling outside the first light of dawn. I rolled over, trying to fall asleep again, but a knocking on the door prevented the prospect of sleeping in. "Argh!" I got out of bed and yelled for whoever it was to come in as I stumbled over to the wardrobe and pulled out a set of clothes, a red button down shirt and a pair of black trousers that had a bunch of buttons instead of a zipper.

I walked into the living area of the suite buttoning my shirt and saw Kai and Mica sitting in two armchairs. "Someone better be dead or dieing, because I really would have liked to have gotten more sleep." I said.

They looked at each other uneasily. "We don't know why we came, we just felt like we had to come see you, and impulse we couldn't get rid of." Mica said, Kai nodding profusely beside him.

"Oh stop nodding Kai, I'm not going to eat your babies or anything, damn." I looked at them, and wondered if my dream last night had anything to do with the impulse they had. "I had a dream last night."

"We all have dreams, Mattes." Kai said.

"Maerik died, again, like he always does, but then," I stopped, trying to find the words. "But then a massive tree, the most beautiful and powerful thing I have ever seen or felt appeared in the center of our old clearing. Its presence in my mind is indescribable, but it gave me some message or something I think."

"You think?" Mica asked, perplexed.

"The words were so definite, like there was power behind them. It said: 'To find me means to find an end, return my stolen gift, and end this blight on spirit and Earth.' I have no idea what it could possibly mean." I told them, taking a seat on the couch in from of them, but standing up again and walking over to a small closet and pulling out a pot and a canister of coarsely ground coffee and three ceramic mugs without handles over to the coffee table.

I filled the pot, which was more or less a French press I had discovered while nosing around the room along with the mugs and coffee, from a pitcher of water. I sat it on the table, and heated it with my fire element. When it was hot I threw a handful of grounds in and let it steep a few moments while I sat back on the couch and studied my friends as they thought about what the tree had told me.

I pressed the plunger down after the smell of delicious coffee started to waft toward my nose and filled the cups, taking one for myself and drinking from it carefully, like a practiced coffee drinker I used the air from my drawing a breath through my mouth to cool the liquid just enough to drink.

"That sounds more like a prophecy than anything, Mattes. But not the prophecy we seek from Cian. What it could mean though, I have no idea." Mica said over his cup.

"Maybe we should tell Jeoffry." I said.

"Perhaps, but I think we had that urge to see you because of what you dreamed of and if it were pertinent for Jeoffry to know, he would be here as well." Mica said.

"We might as well wait and see what Cian says when we find him." Kai said.

"If we find him," I corrected, not so optimistic yet.

"If we find him." Kai agreed.

We finished the pot of coffee, each having two cups or so, and left the cups and pot on the table and went downstairs to the breakfast that had began wafting its way up to us. Ephraim was absent from the table, out making preparations for tomorrow's departure, according to Jeoffry. So we ate in almost total silence except for the occasional requests for bacon, eggs, or potatoes or what have you. Pitchers of juice squeezed from the oranges served yesterday sat on the table and I downed one glass and sipped another with my meal.

After breakfast Jeoffry led us outside to the stables where he showed us the horses we would be riding and how to saddle them as well as how to groom them and ride them. The riding was the most interesting lesson as none of us had ever rode horseback before, having had access to modern marvels such as cars as a means of transportation. It seems here the horse and buggy were ingenious inventions, I couldn't even imagine what these people would think if they had cars.

We each fell off our horses at least once before finally getting the hang of moving with the horse instead of sitting on it like a chair. It was fairly simple after that, but my abs hurt like hell after just a few hours on the horse. When we finally stabled the horses for the night, and brushed them down and took off their saddles, my abs throbbed, my legs ached, and my arms were sore, not to mention the bruises from the various falls through the day.

I plopped on the ground, exhausted from the day, and ready for sleep. "We leave tomorrow at dawn, no?" I asked Jeoffry.

"Yes." Came the short reply.

"Won't you miss your family, your friends? Your home?" I asked him softly.

He remained silent for a while, gazing at the stars that stretched on and on, millions of them, there was no artificial city lighting to pollute the sky here. I could make out several constellations and I'm sure there were millions more in this sky that I'll never know.

"The tree over there," Jeoffry's voice was quiet, and he raised his arm to point to a tree silhouetted in the night. "Its the one my mother planted when I was born. She always told me I'd never be alone as a child, and anytime I wanted to talk to her, I could go to the tree and no matter where she was in the world, she would hear me and comfort me."

"I spent so much time under its bows as a child after she died. Its almost as though she knew she would die, and yet she continued to serve our king. I won't let a fear for death keep me from avenging my mother." We all sat in silence as Jeoffry told us about his mom, and my heart ached for him.

"Do you still see her? In your dreams?" I asked softly, a whisper.

He was silent again and I continued to study the sky while

I waited for him to respond. "She died out here, near her tree. She was picking the ripe fruit from its branches when the Grail's assassins showed up. She fought, but they were too strong, too fast. I watched their dark majick throw her through the air and steal her life." His voice was so full of sorrow I could cut it from his words with a knife. "My father doesn't know, well he suspects, that I saw her die. I see her in my dreams, nightmares mostly, and every time I close my eyes. I see her in every room of the house."

"I see Maerik too, nightmares mostly, some more cruel than the others." I told him just as quietly. Just as sadly. "I see it like a replay of the night we were attacked."

We sat there for a long while and looked at the stars. The sounds the insects made when they chirped reaching my ears. Some looked like little green and yellow stars as they flew around. The bats rustled in the night and screeched their high-pitched trill, finding their way through the night and eating the insects that crossed their path.

It was with some effort that I raised myself from the ground and dragged myself into the house to the dining room where we all ate in total silence and went to bed.

A Journey Begins

Dawn came too soon, though I woke with it, albeit tired. I could feel the subtle aches and pains in my joints and muscles from the previous day's riding lesson. I moaned and groaned my way to the wardrobe putting on the sturdiest looking clothing I could find. I arched my back and stretched my arms and legs, joints gave audible pops here and there to which I sighed, having gained some small modicum of relief from that.

I half expected to hear knocking on the door any second now, as had been the routine the past couple days, but no knocks came. I reached out and brushed Kai and Mica's minds, nudging them awake. I should have marched down the hall and hammered on their doors and jarred them out of sleep for once, but I guess I was feeling nice. Or just too lazy to walk the few steps to their doors. Probably the later.

I felt them grumble out of their slumber and wake. *This is it you guys, today we begin a journey that we may not survive.* I broadcast the thought to them and could feel the twinge of fear leaking through our link. Fear is good though, it will keep us alive, I hope.

Mattes, you never were good at pep talks. Mica's tired thoughts came back to me and I laughed.

Did you expect me to sugar-coat it? I asked. *We may very well not survive, and we need to keep that in mind. Hubris has destroyed a thousand heroes, if I die I want it to be because my opponent is better than me, not because I'm too damn full of myself.*

When you put it that way, I guess it makes sense. It doesn't make you any better at pep talks though. I sent Kai an image of a middle finger and left my room to go downstairs to the dining room.

There was coffee on the table and bowls of fruit,

scrambled eggs, bread, a couple different kinds of butter and cheese, and some juice. I Fixed my coffee with a touch of cream, my absolute favorite way to drink coffee. Cream, real cream not that powdered crap you get at the store, adds a silky richness to coffee that just makes it so much better. The eggs were light and fluffy, and were perfect on the bread with some butter seasoned with thyme and oregano as well as some of the soft cheese spread on it.

The bread itself was amazing, there were little seeds all through it like the rye bread I'm used to, but each time I bit down on one and it popped, a burst of flavor and energy surged through my mouth and body. I was instantly awake and ready to run a marathon, I felt like I could run the entirety of our two week journey in just days, hours, minutes.

Soon the rush of energy wore off slightly, leaving me feeling just better than normal, but still very much awake and eager to go. Kai and Mica joined me along with Jeoffry and Ephraim a few moments after I was finished with my egg sandwich. They sat and piled their plates with eggs, mixing some of the cheese into them.

"Try the bread guys, better than sex." I told them.

"Like you would know." Kai retorted in the most sarcastic tone he could conjure.

"I do, but in case you're wondering, imagine those long showers you take, multiply that by a hundred, and then you have a general idea, this bread is like, a bajillion times better than that." I told him.

Jeoffry smirked suppressing a chuckle, and Ephraim looked taken aback slightly. I guess he was a little more prudish than I thought, but oh well, he'd get over it. "It's ambrosia bread." Ephraim told us, trying to hide his distaste with the direction of the conversation. "The herbs and seeds that go into it are a secret known only to few, the bread itself can take weeks to prepare and gather the ingredients."

Mica took a bite and his eyes popped, "Like a party in my mouth." He said with a mouthful of the stuff. Kai pulled off a chunk and ate it and grabbed some more, not missing a beat or wasting time with talking. They both sat back in their chairs moments later, content and energized by the strange properties of the bread.

We sat there and sipped our coffee, which I noticed had a hint of hazelnut flavor and aroma to it, which I savored.

Ephraim looked strained this morning, the bags under his eyes darker. It looked like he hadn't slept in a couple of days. His forehead was scrunched down in concentration or worry, and a frown was set upon his lips.

"Are you well, Ephraim?" I asked him.

"Well enough, I'm old and tired. There has been little time for rest the last few days, what with preparing this voyage, getting together supplies, contacting my friends in the various cities between here and Schötre." He looked out the windows as he spoke, and I heard the clip clop of horseshoes on cobbled paths before I saw the actual horses come into view.

There were five in all, and they were all linked together with a leader and lead by a stable hand onto the front lawn from the cobbled path leading around the building. "Well, you shouldn't tally any longer. Everything is in order, my cousin Yvette will be expecting you in Giet by sundown." Ephraim stood, chair scraping along the floor as it was pushed back.

"Father, I – " Ephraim started, but was abruptly cut off.

"Do not thank me, Jeoff. I feel as though I've arranged your death and I am not happy with it. Go with my blessing, but do not thank me." Ephraim told his son solemnly.

Thom stood, framed in the door, and walked over and embraced his brother in a strong hug. "Take care Jeoff, be safe, and godspeed."

"Thank you brother." Jeoff said in response, pulling away. "I'll be back, I promise." I wished I could hold the same optimism, but I couldn't. But to try and fail is better than to have never tried at all.

"We should go," I said, standing and moving toward the door. Mica and Kai followed me, Jeoffry too. I could see Ephraim sit back down, and I thought I saw him wipe a tear from his face as he watched us leave.

We walked silently down the halls and out the front door where the four animals stood, bending their heads periodically to graze on the grass below their feet. All four were mares, and chestnut in color, though each had some white markings on them. Between the saddles and the saddle cloths were sandwiched saddlebags stuffed with the various necessities of a trip. We would replenish our supplies at each town or city we were stopped in for a night.

Jeoffry took the lead horse and I the one directly behind him, with Kai behind me and Mica him. "Shall we?" Jeoffry asked.

"Lead the way." I told him, and he nudged his mare into a leisurely trot down the stone cobbled path and out the front gate onto the city road, off in the opposite direction of the bath house. We followed the street through the city, turning down various roads passing many different shops and houses. It was not unlike your average small town, though the shops were a little more specific as to their goods. There were no general stores or anything like that, but fruit stands littered the sides of the streets here and there, some women pedaled their jewelry and pots, down one road was a little outdoor market with tents stretched over wooden poles and goods strewn over makeshift stands or spread over blankets and rugs.

There was an apothecary shop, and even a fortune teller. One building was marked as though it were a pharmacy or a doctor, a stick with a long, dried leathery looking rope twisted around it over the front door. When I asked Jeoffry what it was, his face went cold and he told me it was a surgeon. I shuddered at the thought of surgery without anesthesia and understood Jeoffry's look of horror as goose bumps popped up all down my arms.

After turning down another street, a tall wall appeared in the distance looming over the buildings, we were almost out of Michval. As the wall became closer I could begin to make out a large square cut out of the side and small figures standing to either side. The buildings began to become more and more sparse, mostly houses now.

Jeoffry raised his arm signaling to the pike men to raise their booms and to let us pass and they did. They bowed as we passed, their leader or whatever called "My Lord!" and fisted his chest respectfully as we passed. Jeoffry politely acknowledged them and they lowered their pikes behind us.

The cobbled stone road almost immediately turned to hard packed dirt, grooves dug into either side of the road, likely from farmers carts laden with crops being hauled back into the city for sale and use. Swatches of various crops lined either side of the road and rolled on into the distance, small groves of trees sometimes separating the fields.

When we were about a mile away from the city gates and

the tracts of farmland were starting to break up, Jeoffry nudged his horse into a gallop and we followed suit, keeping up with him as our horses took us over the road as it became rockier and less kept the further we got from the city gates. Trees were begging to pop up more and more frequently until finally that was all we could see for miles around.

We traveled on in this way for many miles, occasionally the path through the trees would split and we would go one way or another, twice we passed little tiny cottages, logs and chopped wood leaning against them, smoke seeping from the chimney, the smell of the night's dinner wafting our direction. When the sun was high in the sky Jeoffry held up a hand and eased his horse into a trot and then a full stop, bringing it around to face us as we did the same.

"We'll stop here and have a bite to eat before we go on." He said when the last of us got stopped and clopped over to stand near him. Jeoffry jumped down from his horse and lead it over to a tree where he looped the reins around it and pulled them taut, showing us how to do the same with our horses.

He pulled out a small round of bread, jerky, and a block of

cheese. The bread was mostly bland and the jerky hard and chewy not very seasoned and the cheese tasted like cheese, but it filled me up and settled my stomach which I was grateful for.

"About how much longer until we reach Giet?" I asked.

"The rest of the day I imagine, we'll probably arrive just before or maybe a little after nightfall." Jeoffry was swatting a fly away from the cheese brick as he answered.

"Well shit." Kai said. "I really have to pee!"

"Really Kai? Really?" I couldn't help but smile at him, and load my voice with as much sarcasm as I could muster. "It's not like you're in the middle of the woods, or anything like that. You don't happen to have a certain piece of equipment or anything like that which enables you to relieve yourself in these situations, or anything like that."

"Oh." Was all he said before stalking off into the woods a modest distance.

"Third tree on the left!" I called after him.

The others laughed quietly at this exchange, continuing to gnaw on their jerky and bread. "What about you guys," Jeoffry asked as Kai rejoined us, retaking his place in the circle. "Wife, kids?"

I laughed at him openly, and swallowed my mouthful of bread and cheese before trying to respond. "Nah, no kids, better not have any brats running around at least."

"Me neither, not much luck in that department." Mica told him.

Kai didn't respond, and I had to suppress a smile. "Oh come on Kai! There's no way in hell you could have landed her, way out of your league." I told him.

"Is he still moping about Lisa?" Mica asked.

"Well, I guess I'll never know now, will I?" Kai responded.

$"Oh you know damn well that it would have went down like 'Aw hell naw.'" Mica told him. "We're not going anywhere for a few thousand years, plenty of girls in this decade."

"And you know what, I'm sure they even have prostitutes in this time too, just in case." I said in mock seriousness.

"If by prostitute you mean someone who takes money for sexual favors, then yeah, we got those." Jeoffry explained.

"Sexual favors? Don't be a prude, Jeoffry, they take money for hot, sweaty, disease ridden sex and fake every minute of it." The piece of bread in my hand fell into my lap as I fell back, laughing at Mica's comment. "What did I say?"

"What didn't you say?" I answered his question with a question between bursts of laughter. "With you here, we can afford to be a little prudish."

"Hey, I call it how I see it." He said back with that grin I'm accustomed to seeing on him.

"Right guys, if we want to get a good bed at an inn we need to get moving. We still have about three leagues between us and Giet to cross." Jeoffry hopped to his feet. "You can eat in the saddle, we need to get moving, we'll take dinner at the city."

Jeoffry set the pace at a hard gallop and we rode hard, diving through the trees, whipping between and around them dangerously as we went. I quickly realized that the whole eating in the saddle thing was not going to happen if I were to stay on my horse so I ditched the remaining chunk of jerky I had and took the reins in both hands.

I almost ran into at least two trees before finding a rhythm and began to steer more instinctively. After about 2 hours of hard riding we were out of the trees for the most part and running through a grassy field, the tall stocks of grass coming up to my knees.

The openness of the field was short lived however as after a few moments the trees began to spring up again on the other side and Jeoffry plowed on. We were back to weaving through the trees again, the horses were beginning to tire slightly, I could feel them starting to respond a little slower, and I was beginning to hear their breathing over the thundering of hooves.

I noticed a small stream ahead and so did Jeoffry apparently, or maybe he just knew it was there. Either way he held up a hand, motioning for us to stop and began to slow his own horse, jumping off as it came to a stop and leading it to the edge of the stream.

The horses gulped down the water, and relieved themselves as they drank. We followed suit, cupping water in our hands and bringing it to our mouths and slurping it down, the sun was beginning to wane from the afternoon sky and I was hot and sticky from the hot, humid air, so I splashed some of the cold spring water over my face and head.

We were soon riding through the trees again, though a little more moderately paced. I could see the trees starting to thin as time wore on and finally we were out of the trees and moving over a seriously rough path we had picked up in the woods. Far off in the distance thin streamers of smoke could be seen wafting into the sky, hardly even noticeable.

The sun was just over the horizon, the sky turning a deep red and purple in the sunset. As we rode the path grew no less rocky, however the gates of Giet began to become visible growing clearer every minute. Soon the sun sank below the horizon and less than a quarter of an hour later we skidded to a stop at the gates of Giet.

Two massive wooden doors towered above, iron strips reinforcing the logs and holding them more securely together. "Oh fuck me! Fuck me!" Jeoffry was saying from the back of his horse before jumping down and running over to the doors, beating on them with his fist.

"Open the gates! Open these damn gates!" He yelled loudly.

112

"Yer ought be knowin' better me lad." A voice called back. "The gates close ah sun don."

"Shit!" Jeoffry said softly, then to us, "I forgot about this stupid city's lockout policy."

"Now what?" I asked him, unsure what we should do. I really was not looking forward to sleeping on the hard ground, not tonight, there was plenty of time for that later.

"Now he's going to open those damn gates if he knows what's good for him." Jeoffry growled, anger touching his voice. He turned toward the gates and hollered over again. "Open these gates, that's an order soldier!"

"I cannah do that laddy. Yer be knowin the rules. And I be a sergeant ter yeh lad." The voice called back.

"You'll be a private with my foot up your ass if these gates don't open!" Jeoffry yelled back. "I am Jeoffry of Michval, and I command it!"

"Ah, well, in tha' case me lad, yeh shoul' ave said som'thin sooner!" The voice yelled and footsteps could be heard on the other side, running around, working levers and wheels, and slowly the gates opened inward.

113

Jeoffry walked his horse through and went up to a the soldier who was clearly the only one who could be called a sergeant given his uniform, and grabbed him up by the collar. "I bear this land's Salvation, come after centuries the Chosen Three are on a quest to rid the land of Marqus' evil and darkness!" His voice was once again coming out as a growl. And the soldier was shaking a bit, eyes as wide as a deer caught in your headlights.

"I-I-I didnah be knowin who ye were me Lord." He said shakily. "Thought ye be sum o' th' vagrants that be movin' into th' city lately."

"I'll forgive you for your ignorance, but do not let it happen again." Jeoffry said, stepping away from him.

"You scared the shit out of him." I told him as we walked away.

"No, not me, you. All three of you." He said.

"Why would he be scared of us?" I asked. "We're supposed to be here to help people, not destroy them."

"Not of you specifically, but of your power. The Chosen are supposed to possess immense power. Enough to bring down

114

cities like this without breaking so much as a sweat." He explained. "The Trincan Elder were not always good, Matthias. Our scrolls and books speak of Elder Trincan who went rogue, and the destruction and devastation they caused was immense."

"Oh." Was all I could say. I couldn't imagine Elder Trincan going rogue, but I guess even in the most ancient of times, people were susceptible to embracing the evil inside them, inside all of us.

Jeoffry led us down the unfamiliar. narrow streets, turning here and there, toward an unknown destination. We were soon outside a smallish building, loud noises coming from inside. We tied our horses to a rail, and went inside.

The sound of drunkards and gambling and drunken laughter bombarded the air and filled my ears. There were small tables with chairs around them spread through the room, a small bar on the wall opposite the door, and a fireplace on the wall to the right of the bar. Jeoffry led us to the bar and after some time got the woman behind the bar's attention. I assumed this was Yvette when heard him ask if she still had our room available and if someone could take care of our horses.

"I have one room left, and a stable boy can attend your horses." I heard her say over the obnoxious noise of the place through an accent not unlike the southern accent common in the southern states in our own time.

Jeoffry handed her a small handful of gold coins and she gave him a iron skeleton key, three bowls and three carved wooden soup spoons. He got us to follow him over to the hearth where a huge pot of thick, creamy potato soup simmered over the flames. He took the ladle off the hook, filled his bowl and passed it to me and went to sit down on the other side of the room in the corner, far away from the hot fireplace.

We each joined him in turn and sat down at the table in the wooden chairs that were parked there. The soup was delicious and satisfying after the meager lunch we ate on the trail. Soon my bowl was empty and I was sitting back in my chair, full and content, and feeling pretty tired.

"So," I asked. "Where do we go after this?"

"We go to Phlenyl, about two days out from the capital."

He answered, pushing his bowl back and waving down the bar maid. She came over and he asked for something to drink, the three of us got coffees with cream, and Jeoffry got what equated to a glass of beer, and probably tasted as bad too.

"How do you stomach that shit?" I asked rhetorically. "So, how far from here to Phlenyl?"

He thought about it for a moment, took a sip of his beer, grimaced slightly to which I grinned, and answered. "A few days if we don't cut out to any of the smaller villages along the way. As we get closer to the capital estate the trees start to dissipate and the terrain is flatter, mostly open plains.

"From there we cross the Bvoten river, and continue east to Ashara and north to Schötre." Jeoffry continued after another drink of his beer.

"And then we look for Cian." I said.

"Yes, then we look for Cian--" Jeoffry was cut short by a shrill yell.

"Let me go!" Could be heard over the laughter and noise of the room. I stood, to try and get a better look, and saw some drunk guy grab a woman's wrist. She was trying to pull free of his strong hand when she swatted at him. She landed a solid punch to his face, which caused his lip to crack open and a drop of blood began to form there.

He licked his lip and his eyes got wilder, and he yelled at her. "You dirty little whore!" His hand swung back, ready to strike her hard and square across her face and that's when I'd had enough. I reacted quickly, before I even knew what I was doing. I knocked my chair back and it hit the floor with a loud thunk.

I flung my hand out had him, sending air after that hand, holding it from moving even an inch. "Let her go." I said calmly, and stepped around the fallen chair. I pushed through the now quiet room toward the idiot and the woman.

"Who the hell are you?" The man growled.

"Someone with a little more respect for others than yourself. I won't ask again." I said back, still doing my best to keep my voice and my mind calm so I could control my hold on the air stopping his hand. There was a look of horror and shock at the woman's face.

"You have naught to do with this lad, mind your own." He said, while he struggled against the air that held his arm. "Let me go and I'll forgive your indiscretion!"

"You all heard me warn him." I said a little more loudly, to anyone who was listening, which was just about everyone with ears in the room. I walked over to him, and wrapped my arm around the woman he was holding tight to, and placed my hand over his. I manipulated the heat in the room, concentrating it at the palm of my hand, slowly I increased the intensity of the heat there, until at last I smelled singed hair and he yelped and snatched his hand back. The woman stumbled back and I held her, letting her get her footing before pushing her behind me.

"Please don't try anything stupid, I hope that's not asking too much." I said, releasing my hold on his other arm.

He immediately leaped from his chair, it flew back and fell over. As he reached me my arm curled up, my hand clenched into a fist, level with his solar plexus. Just before he would have ran into my fist, I imagined my hand pushing straight through his body and out the other side as I stepped forward and pushed my arm out slightly, making contact with the area

119

between his gut and his chest using his momentum to power the blow.

He fell to the floor on the spot, gasping for air, curling into the fetal position. I turned, and walked back to our table, picked up my chair, and sat down, drinking the last of my coffee, leaving a bit at the bottom which had a few dregs of coffee grounds in it. I couldn't help but find myself wondering if these people knew about coffee filters.

"Thank you." was a soft voice behind me.

I turned, startled, and saw the same woman from before. "You shouldn't have done that." She told me.

"Why shouldn't I stop a pompous ass like him from hitting someone such as yourself?" I wondered aloud to her.

"He's the leader of a gang of ruffians just like him." She told me. "He'll bring all his friends after you. Next time, it won't just be him."

"Let him." I said.

"You're not from around here, are you?" She asked.

"You could say that." I told her. "But I'm not afraid of a

bunch of women beating punks, either."

"Just so that you know what you're bargaining for." She said. "It could be your life." With that she walked away and slipped out the front door as the big guy got off the floor. Noise levels had returned to normal by now, and I was mildly aware of the guy recovering slightly, as he staggered over toward us.

"I really don't want to hurt you." I told him when I knew he was close enough to hear me. "I will, but I don't want to. Just leave."

"You'll regret this lad, mark my words you will. And next time your little majick tricks won't help you either." He stomped off out the door one arm cradling his stomach.

"Congratulations." Jeoffry said to me. "You've been in this city for only a few hours and you've already pissed some dangerous people off."

"I've been attacked by a horde of dark majicians and lived, I'm not afraid of that lot." I told him.

"I hope you know to be careful. You're not invincible Matthias." Jeoffry said. "Be careful of whom you cross."

"Right." I said, exaggerating a yawn. "I'm really tired, and I suppose we'll be getting off early tomorrow."

"We will." Jeoffry drained the last bit of his beer and stood. "Let's go see if we can't find our room."

There was a stairwell set into the wall to the left of the bar. We climbed up it one floor and and followed the hall at the top of the landing. We tried the key the woman gave Jeoffry in every door along the way until we found the room it opened and went inside. There was one bed in the middle of the room, just big enough for two people to fit comfortably. To one side was a small, and I do mean small, stand with a lantern sitting on it. Kai walked over to it, lifted the globe and turned up the wick a bit. He lit it with some channeled fire energy. When the lamp burned brightly enough, I closed the door and blocked out the light from the lamps on the wall.

"Who gets the bed?" I asked.

"Rock, Paper, Scissors." Mica said. After teaching Jeoffry how to play, we played for best two out of three, and unfortunately I lost, along with Kai. Mica was always too good at this game, and it would seem Jeoffry had a good stroke of beginners' luck.

"I hope you don't mind, but I sleep nude." Mica said doing his best to look serious.

"Like hell you do." Jeoffry said, though I'm not sure because of the light, but I could swear he blushed a bit.

Mica laughed heartily and crawled into the bed on the side with the lantern, Jeoffry climbing in on the other side.

Kai and I both found spots on the floor, it was decided we would get the pillows since they got the bed, so at least my head was cushioned well. I fell asleep quickly and for once, I slept soundly, no dreams, no waking in a cold sweat in the middle of the night, no prophecies. Just deep, dark sleep. The only thing that upset me was being shaken awake by Jeoffry in the morning, if that's what you call it. The sun had yet to come up, a sliver of the moon was still visible over the horizon. I think it's worth noting that the moon is huge here. So huge on the horizon, in fact, that it's almost as if you could get there fast enough, before the night ends, you could reach out over that line and touch it.

Dreaming

We had the horses saddled and were on our way out of the city, turning back along the way we'd come. Jeoffry made the final turn that would put us on the road that led to the gate when he pulled back on the reins, bringing his mount to a sudden halt, rearing on it's hind legs a little bit. I stopped a little slower, though still too fast for the the horse's liking and it neighed unpleasantly at me, and snorted a jet of steam from its nostrils in the brisk morning air.

"What the hell." I wondered aloud at the thirty odd people blocking our path.

"Move aside, let us pass!" Jeoffry called to them.

"I warned ye laddy!" Came a familiar voice from the middle

of the front line. He stepped out of the line a bit, away from the group, and I recognized him as the lunatic from last night.

"Look, we don't want to fight, we just want to be on our way." I called over to him. Did this guy have you-know-what for brains? Actually, I'd be willing to wager he didn't have anything up there, period.

"Can we just burn them and be done with it?" Kai asked, clearly not serious but the idea was tempting nonetheless.

"As tempting as that sounds, let's try not to kill any of them unless they don't give us the option." I told them. "Frankly, I'm hoping the Brainless One up front does just that, he's really starting to piss me off."

"Your little tricks got me lad, but will they work on the lot o' us? Eh?" He called over to us.

"Honestly, 'little tricks?' I find that ever so slightly insulting. We don't have time for this bullshit. Let's just push through, try not to hurt them, just push them back with air or something." I gave the instructions and nudged my horse forward into a trot, urging it into a gallop.

I saw a few in the back with knocked bows, and I willed

126

the air around us to solidify and push the arrows around our group. The whole front row ran at us with knives and spears and swords and axes raised. I tripped as many as I could with blocks of dirt and stone I raised from the ground beneath their feet. Many of them fell, but a few kept coming or were able to catch their balance.

One with a sword was right in front of me, poised to strike and I threw out my fist tossing him back with a gust of air I gathered from around us and solidified with some of my own earth energy.

This is taking far too long, you guys. I thought to the other two.

What else can we do without hurting them? Kai asked.

I'm going to try to put together a temporary spell that will hold them in place for a bit, long enough for us to be on our way at the least. I started to focus on the ground under their feet, infusing it with some of the water energy I drew from my core. *I hope this works.* I thought across our link.

I willed the ground under them to become liquid, feeding my will into the majick. I willed it to become liquid, and they all sank into the ground up to their chests, and I changed the flow of energy and followed it with a command to harden. I added a command to the will of the majick to release them when we were sufficiently far away.

With each command, I fed the spell with some of my own stored energy and I could feel those stores becoming smaller, albeit slightly, but I could feel the drain on my energy nonetheless.

I dismounted my horse and led it through the mass of chests and heads, muttering a "Pardon me!" here and an "Excuse me, sir!" there, as much as I hate to admit it, I was enjoying this. A lot. There were cries of frustration, pleas for us to let them free, some groaned and grunted as they strained against the ground trying to push their way free.

When we were all across the field of torsos, we mounted up and rode off through the gate, the guards moving out of our way quickly, probably afraid of becoming human trees themselves. When we were a safe distance from the city, we slowed down to a more leisurely pace, and I heard Kai yell back to me, "That was so freaking awesome man!"

"Will they be okay?" Jeoffry asked me.

"Yeah. The ground will free them when we're too far away to be followed." I told him. "Are people usually that damned stupid?"

"A few." He replied. "That particular idiot was the Count's nephew. Which means the normal rules don't really apply to him, just as they don't always apply to me. Some of the nobles abuse that, and some accept it as a responsibility."

"I suppose he's one of the former." I said. It was not a question.

"You noticed." Jeoffry answered anyway. "That was some pretty crafty work you did back there."

"Thanks." I told him.

"Well, no doubt the kingdom knows now that the Chosen have arrived, or are at least suspecting as much." Jeoffry informed us. "Unfortunately, that also means our enemies know you're here."

"So then let them come!" I said coldly. "I won't show them the same mercy I showed the clouded men in the city."

"No doubt, but Mattes, understand that you are not a god, and that someone may be able to best you." Jeoffry pulled his horse up to face me and stopped, and spoke in a soft, serious voice. "Keep your wits about you, and know humility if you hope to survive. We are up against some of the darkest and most powerful people to walk this ground. Matthias there are more of them, than there are us. You can't sink them all into the ground."

"'I'll show you fear in a handful of dust,' I'm not afraid of death, Jeoffry. I'm afraid of being forgotten when I die. I plan to live a life that is unforgettable, one that is noble." I nudged my horse and set it back into a trot, pushing past Jeoffry. He made a clicking sound and rode up to take his spot leading the way.

"You didn't come up with that by yourself, did you?" Jeoffry asked me.

"No," Mica spoke up. "He was quoting T.S. Elitott, he doesn't exist yet but he will be an amazing writer."

We were silent for a while, no sound but the wind blowing over the grassy plains splitting around us. Hooves clomped on the soft dirt, muffled by the grass below. Birds could be seen overhead gliding on currents of warm air. Something with antlers, a deer perhaps, bounded over the plain, it

130

leaped through the grass and bobbed up and down like a dolphin through the ocean.

We ate some bread and cheese in the saddle, not wanting to stop for lunch and loose time. We took a much more leisurely pace toward Phlenyl, the horses would die of exertion halfway there if we rode them as hard as we did to Giet.

My butt was starting to ache from sitting in a saddle for these extended periods. I wondered if Jeoffry had a callous on his butt, but didn't say anything, though I did laugh silently to myself. I considered for a moment hopping off my horse and running along side it for a while, but decided that would slow us down too much. Plus the sun was just now beginning to sink from the sky and was level with my face, beating down on me. I figured I'd probably die of a heat stroke or something if I ran now. I began to wonder if they had some equivalent to sunscreen here, because I was seriously beginning to think that I was going to be very well done and beet-red if we continued riding right under the sun like this. Given the almost total lack of trees, I was beginning to understand that shade was an unfamiliar term to this area.

As the fiery ball of scorching heat sunk toward the horizon, the air began to cool the sweat pouring down my face, and soaking my hair. I savored every gentle blow and sighed with relief, in unison with the gentle breeze. The sun sank lower and lower with each passing moment. It lit up the horizon in the most beautiful sunset streaked with purples and reds and blues.

We stopped shortly before dark and walked the horses in a large circle to stomp down the grass so that we could set up camp for the night. We all unsaddled our horses and brushed them down with the brushes from our saddle bags. I combed the burrs and pieces of leaves and grass from my horses tail. It whinnied once and sidestepped when a burr got tangled in the long tail hair and I had to tug a bit to get it out.

With the horses taken care of and left to munch on some of the grass, Jeoffry walked off into the sea of grassy fields and left us to set a fire in our little clearing. Mica waved his hand over the ground near the center of the crude circle and a small hole began to boil into existence. I say boil because if you have ever seen a pot of potatoes boiling, and saw how the white foamy stuff floating on top moves to the edge of the pot, then you know what this looked like. The dirt stirred and broke apart at the epicenter of the hole and began to spread out, pushing the dislocated dirt to the edge and then out over to cover the grass around the hole protecting it from sparks. Strangely enough, there was some wood littered here and there about the ground, which we set to gathering. There wasn't all that much, but we managed to find some well seasoned, gnarled pieces of wood that were probably from uprooted trees blown over in the wind blowing across the plains during a storm.

We each gathered a modest armful of the gnarled wood and tossed it onto a pile off to the side and stacked a few pieces in the earthen hole, lined it with some dried grass and small sticks that were shaved with a knife so that thin pieces of the wood curled up from them.

When everything was in place, Mica crossed his fingers and shot a spark from his finger at the base of the small pile where the grass and shaved sticks lay. By the time Jeoffry returned, the sun had fully set from the sky and it was almost completely dark. The eerie sounds of night reched my ears along with the crackling and popping of the fire as it burned away.

He carried three small rabbits that had been cleaned and skinned. He found a large flat stone and lay it over some coals he raked out with a stick. When the stone was hot he placed the now quartered meat on them and lay some herbs he'd found on the searing meat.

As the fat pooled on the stone and ran off into the coals, jets of flame would shoot up, lighting the clearing brightly then dying down. The aromas of cooking meat began to fill my senses. I could hear the sizzling of it cooking in its fat as it dripped off the stone. The smell of it mingled with the herbs reached my nose. Soon a golden color began to appear on the surface of the pieces on the stone as they cooked and my mouth began to water. Jeoffry grabbed some bread from a saddle bag and we ate.

Feeling ravenous from the heat I devoured one piece without even tasting it, then another, periodically taking a bite of the hard bread as well. Feeling stuffed, my hunger satiated, I rolled out my bedroll and lay down, exhausted. Sleep came almost immediately even on the rough ground where I could feel every uneven spot beneath the padding of the grass and my roll.

A dark clad figure stood on the edge of a cliff, his black and red robes billowing in the wind. A long, curved sword hung from his hip, and his arms were folded behind his back. He looked at me from beneath the hood, most of his face cast in shadow, his eyes barely visible. I could feel them burning into me at any rate, and it made me wary, the way he stared.

"Align with darkness and live away from fear." The hooded figure said.

I could barely move my lips to speak, but managed to choke out a gasping "No." I then noticed the tendril of darkness twining up my leg, grabbing hold of me and slithering up my body, wrapping around my neck and making it hard to breath. I forced the purest kind of energy I could gather from my center and radiated it out. The soft glow it created around me forced the dark tendrils to slink away, back to the hooded figure, where it coalesced in his shadow and hid there.

There were people everywhere, lined up in rows, all in black, and I was in a cave now, hiding in a corner. There was a bunch of static noise and voices and I couldn't pick anything in particular out. I tried to move closer, to hear what those closest to me were saying, but the closer I got, the louder the noise got, but no one voice stuck out above the rest.

It was obvious no one understood I was there, whether I was anywhere remained to be seen. But as I moved around the cloaked figures, I noticed a statuesque quality about them before understanding that they were in fact statues themselves.

I moved through and a round them, trying to find some way out of this nightmare. I soon arrived at the center of a massive circle of people. And again I was somewhere else, this time chaotic and screaming everywhere. I pushed myself off the grass which was burned and trampled and wet in some places with blood. I saw someone rush toward me. I waved my hand through the air like I would bring my arm across his throat and he fell to the ground.

I knew where I was and what was happening before I realized it consciously. I was once more in the circle where my life fell apart and everything I loved was destroyed. I saw Maerik's final battle and ran over to help him. His adversary burned a fiery death as the dagger appeared again from

Maerik's chest and I caught him, out of habit, and helped him to the ground where I knew he would die.

And again there was the tree, glowing soft, wisps fluttering around it and through its branches. Everything was gone and it was just me and this tree in the middle of a massive field, surrounded by the darkness of night.

I knew there was something special about the tree, it wasn't as if there was some terrible trauma in my past with a giant glowing spirit-like tree like I'd had with evil people in black robes. So I knew it wasn't just a a coincidence that I was seeing the same tree in my dreams at night, and sometimes hearing it broadcasting messages through my mind. I opened up the barrier that I kept blocking my consciousness and waited. But there was nothing for a while, I just sat there admiring the being, it had to be some kind of being, not just a tree.

The image of this thing before me sent chills down my neck and up my arms. It awed me, and inspired a sense of safety and strength and a warmth that spread from my chest outward within me.

You must seek me child

137

When it is time, you shall know.
Come to me at your time of need,
and I will give you the gift that is mine to give.

The voice I heard when it spoke in my head was lyrical and eloquent. I sat there trying to comprehend what it meant when I woke to someone poking me gently in the side. "Matthias, wake up. We need to be off."

"Go to hell." I mumbled and turned over, trying to find sleep again.

"Now, Matthias! Wake up!" I rolled over and saw a vision of Jeoffry, blurred by sleep.

"Argh!" I groaned and sat up, rubbing the sleep from my eyes and blinking. "It's still dark."

"It's only a short while before sunrise" Jeoffry replied. "Get up and get your stuff together."

I stood and stretched, exaggerated a loud yawn, making it clear that I was still very much tired. Bending over I rolled up my ground cloth and tied it tight with a small piece of robe and then onto the saddle with a pair of leather thongs.

With some effort I heaved the saddle over my horse's back

and strapped it on tight, making sure it was snug so it didn't slide around and chafe the horse or slide to the side so I fell off. We broke camp, filled in the hole we built the fire in, and rode off.

Destined Enemies

The trip to Phlenyl was long and exhausting. We rode for nearly a week across a long stretch of grassland. The region itself very plain and completely uneventful. I thought it was just going to be a two day venture, but I misunderstood Jeoffry. It would take us nearly two weeks to get to the capital, which we would pass and continue on for two days to Phlenyl. After the second day of riding I was bored, and tired. We almost never ate breakfast to conserve what little food we could carry. Lunch was always ate in the scorching sun, and dinner, if I was awake enough to eat it, was usually bread and cheese or jerky unless Jeoffry managed to kill something.

We generally didn't make camp for the majority of the trip

until after sundown when we could no longer see to know where we were going, and we always woke just before sun up and started moving again by the scant light from the moon just above the horizon and the tell tale luminescence just below the horizon of the impending sunlight.

By the time we arrived at the city gates, we were all very much tanned, our clothes worn, and clearly in need of a hot bath and for some of us a shave.

I was plagued by nightmares the entirety of the way, and as the days wore on I became more and more on edge and anxious. A weird feeling began to build as we got closer to Phlenyl and nothing I did was able to dispel it. I felt as though we should just continue past Phlenyl but that wasn't possible. We needed some rest, food, clothes, and if I didn't get to bathe soon, I would probably itch my scalp off.

We stabled our horses at a small stable just inside the city, and went off in search of a place to bathe. Jeoffry hadn't been here since he was a young child and didn't know the place well, and ended up asking a footman directions. The guard gave very animated directions to Jeoffry who led us off down the streets toward the other side of the city.

142

Clothes were strung high above the streets on lines fed through metal eyelets on the buildings on either side high above the ground. Children ran and played in the streets, tossing around the inflated bladder of some animal, probably a pig, or playing soldier with sticks. Others played their version of tag, or leap frog.

Their shrill laughter reminded me of how much I hate kids. My achy, tired body didn't make my mood any better. One little boy however, was a little different from the rest. I watched as he walked up to the group of kids playing with their ball, and snatched it away from them. He ran across the street and down a small ally that was actually just a recess in the wall and tried to hide. The other kids weren't fooled however, and ran after him and tried to follow him into the recess to get their ball back from the little brat.

When the boy whose ball he apparently took tried to step into the alcove, he was stopped dead by an invisible wall. The little prat has a gift for majick, and he decides to use it to bully the other little kids. "Give us our ball back you freak!" The boy who tried to go after the ball yelled.

"I'm telling your mom Jodah!" A little girl yelled and ran off down the street screaming after the boys mother. They both returned seconds later, the mother screaming at the child to come out.

"If you don't come out of there this instant Jodah, oh!" The woman gasped as an invisible force buffeted her back and she fell, landing on her butt in the middle of the street.

I started to move forward but Mica put a hand on my shoulder. "Sorry mate, but you've never been good with kids. You might strangle the little brat."

"That's an understatement if I ever heard one." Kai said as Mica walked on ahead of me.

"I. Will. Not. Have. Kids." I said through gritted teeth.

Jeoffry left us standing there and walked over and helped up the mother and brought her back to where Kai and I were standing. "He's not usually like this." She started.

"Save it." I told her harshly. "Your kid is a bully, and selfish. But worst of all, he's using his gift for personal gain and to hurt other innocent people."

"I don't know what to do with him." She sobbed.

"Beat the shit out of him and send his ass to bed, that's what you do with him." I told her.

"You don't understand, what he just did is nothing really. We can't control him anymore." I could barely understand her through her crying.

Mica was standing in front of the recess now, pushing on the barrier. It was solid, and impassible. I saw him raise his hands, and place the tips of his fingers and thumbs on the barrier. His eyes closed and a soft glow formed under his palms. A few seconds later he lowered his arms and moved past the invisible wall.

He came out carrying a ball in one hand which he tossed to the kid who was yelling at the boy before. In his other hand was the arm of the brat, whose name was apparently Jodah. He kicked and screamed the whole way over to us. He yelled something about making us pay or that we'll be sorry.

I felt little bursts, or touches on the metaphysical shield I kept around me, protecting me from most basic majickal attacks. I was kind of intrigued at his well developed ability at such a young age, and yet afraid for what he would one day become, and the power I knew he would one day wield, if he

145

continued down the same path he was on now.

I looked the kid in the eye when he stood in front of me beside Mica, and held my hand out in front of him. There at the center, grew a very hot, very dangerous, very deadly ball of fire. "Look kid, using your gifts to hurt people is not what they were intended for. If we were given gifts to hurt people, you would be a pile of ashes on the ground over there." I flung the hand holding my fireball toward the place he was hiding before. The fire disappeared just as it left the slightest scorch mark on the ground.

I stared at him and watched as his eyes got big and followed the fireball to where it landed on the ground. "Can you show me how to do that?" He asked, awed.

Mica squatted down in front of Jodah holding his shoulder tightly. "No, we can not." He told him firmly and continued on with the same serious voice. "Jodah, I need you to understand that being mean, and using your gifts to be mean and hurt people is bad. I need you to promise me you won't do that anymore."

"I promise." He said quietly.

"I really hope you mean that." Mica told him. "Because us three," Mica pointed to Kai and myself. "We are good guys, and it's our job to protect good people and destroy bad people. If you keep doing bad stuff with your gift, we'll have no choice but to destroy you, too. And we don't want to do that. Everyone creates their own destiny. What will yours be, helping people, or hurting them and living in fear, wondering when we will come to stop you?"

"I–I want to help people." He said softly, hanging his head.

"Good." Mica told him.

We left the brat and his mother and continued down the end of the street and turned right onto a road lined with mostly businesses and shops. People coming and going from the various buildings doing their errands. "I still think we should have just killed the kid."

"Mattes!" Mica yelled at me.

"What?" I said. "He clearly has no respect for others."

"He said he'll be nice." Kai pointed out.

"Kai, you told the principal you would behave yourself and not try beating Mica up how many times?" I reminded him.

147

"Oh. That was different." He said.

"Really?" I asked. "You only stopped because I made you two play nice or I wasn't going to have anything to do with either of you. I'm thinking that kid doesn't have that kind of catalyst."

"No, but he'll probably have nightmares of a big mangy man throwing fire balls all over the damn place." Mica cut in.

"He deserves it." I rebutted.

"Shall we continue?" Jeoffry butt in before we could argue any longer.

"Yes, let's" I said and followed Jeoffry down the street. He led us down several turns and I think he got us lost once but Jeoffry quickly righted his path and we were off again.

Soon we were at a large square building but the road didn't split around it, it stopped here. The bath house was at the end of a cul-de-sac with a small statue of a young male, an endless stream of water mimicking urine splashing into the pool below. Some greenery lined the path but is was no where near as eloquent and beautiful as the entry to the bath house back in Michval.

Inside we stripped and hopped into the pool quickly. I used some of the energy swarming around in the hot water to replenish by body. I relaxed into the water as the heat soothed the aches in my joints and released the tension from body.

"How long are we here?" I asked Jeoffry, not particularly eager to be moving again.

"A day, two, at the most. Long enough to rest and get supplies together." He said to me.

I laid back and rested my body for a while before I scrubbed the dirt and grime from my hair and skin. Dead skin cells floated across the surface of the water. I got out and toweled off, putting on a pair of white linen pants and loose v-neck shirt of the same fabric. The outfit was cool and breathable in the dry heat outside.

We made our way to the center of the town where a large house or small mansion stood. The doorway was vaulted up into a point, and split open at the center. Two large brass rings hung as door handles from other slab of polished oak making up the doors themselves. Jeoffry raised and dropped a large knocker on the right door frame several times. Each

149

rap of the metal ball on the knocking plate echoed around us and reverberated through the house, I'm certain.

Moments later a tall man dressed in formal-looking clothes opened the door and motioned us in. "What you can I do for you gentlemen?" The man asked us.

"I'm Lord Jeoffry of Michval the Younger, son of His Majesty Prince Ephraim of Michval. I'm here on business and have decided to visit my Cousin. Is he here?" Jeoffry asked.

"Forgive me my Lord." The tall guy fisted his chest and bowed slightly. "Yes, come this way, and I'll let him know you are here." He left us in a small comfortable room and bode us help ourselves to something to drink off a small, but expensive looking, bar on a stand in the back corner.

No one moved for a drink, and a larger man walked in. He looked like he may have one day been youthful and fit, but the years had left him rotund. He wore elegant sapphire robes trimmed with gold and silver filigree. "Jeoff, my boy! I haven't seen you since you were a mere child." The man lowered his hand to somewhere above his knee for emphasis. "You have grown into a fine young man. How's your father?"

"He is well." Jeoffry responded. "How are you Cousin Logan?"

"Good, good!" Logan replied in turn. "And who do we have here? Not your siblings, I don't see the family resemblance anywhere."

"Look closely and you shall know the truth uncle, which is why I am here in Phlenyl and why I must ask of a boon from you Cousin." Jeoffry told him.

"What are you on about?" He questioned, looking us up and down. He did a double take and focused on my neck. "It can't be."

"Yes, Cousin, the Chosen have arrived." Jeoffry told him.

"You're sure?" He questioned skeptically.

"Positive, they're Trincan, and of the Elder race." He confirmed.

"The Gods bless you." Logan said to us, fisting his chest and kneeling before me.

"That's not necessary my Lord." I told him.

"I see." Logan said, standing again. "What will you have of

me cousin? If it is in my power it will be done."

"Incidents in Giet make me wary of procuring a room at the inn or pub." He explained my run-in with the brutish womanizer and the stand they made at our departure. "I would be honored if you would allow us to remain here for a day, two, at the most."

"The honor is mine, cousin. To have you and those of the Trincan Elder race in my home at the same time is a high honor indeed." Logan told us. He opened a small panel on the wall to the right of the door and reached in and pulled a cord. A clanging in the back of the house could be heard softly.

Moments later a beautiful young girl about eighteen or so walked through the door and curtsied low. I thought I saw Kai's jaw drop and eyes pop]slightly, but he regained his composure quickly and nobody else seemed to notice. I smiled to myself and shook my head slightly catching Kai's eye. He gave me that "What" look and I gave him a "You know what" look in return.

"My Lord." The girl said. She seemed to be looking at Kai as she said it. Kai was completely focused on ogling her like some prize.

"Show these boys to the guest suite and make sure they're well fed." Logan told her. "Jeoff, I would be delighted if you would stay and talk with me for a moment longer. I know your journey has been long, but there is so much to catch up on and I would hate to bore these young fellows with family affairs." I was sure he was more interested in prying as much information from Jeoffry as he could about us and cared little about old news of his distant relatives.

"Of course my Lord." She said, and beckoned us after her.

Kai leaped from his seat and walked beside her, Mica and I followed behind. Kai engaged her in what I hoped was some polite conversation, I heard her giggle a couple times at his apparently witty topic. We soon arrived in a small kitchen where we stopped.

There was a table and bench in the far corner. We sat down as the girl moved around the room gathering a few things from shelves including a small pot, she disappeared into a small pantry on the right wall and emerged with some potatoes and what appeared to be a picture of cream. She peeled the potatoes and cubed them as we watched, tossing them into the pot along with dried pork she heated in a skillet and diced. The cream as well as a bit of some liquid that was already steaming over the fire went in next.

She struggled to lift the pot from the island to the hearth and Kai hurried over to lend a hand to her efforts, removing one pot from the hook over the fire and replacing it with the new one full of what I presumed to be a potato stew. When steam started to roll off the top of the pot, the girl tossed in some herbs she gathered from the garden just outside the door.

"Have a seat Delia." Kai motioned to an empty spot on the bench beside him.

"I see you two have been acquainted." I mumbled softly.

"You're just jealous." He said back quietly.

"Not in the least." Mica and I said almost at the same time.

Delia looked a little apprehensive, but Kai reassured her the world wouldn't end if the maid sat down for a few minutes. "Delia, this is Mica, and that's Matthias." He told her. We each nodded our heads as he introduced us to his girlfriend slash crush slash something.

"What's so funny Mattes?" Kai asked, confused.

"Nothing." I lied. I guess Kai is a bit of a player, news to me I thought. Though I wondered why I hadn't noticed this before. I'd like to think it was because the girls in our time had some common sense and didn't fall for the tricks guys like Kai liked to use.

"It's getting late." I announced after we'd ate. I noticed the room being much darker than earlier and from the window I could see the sun settling below the horizon inch by inch. "Its been a long couple of days, and a warm, soft bed sounds extremely nice right now."

"I can show you to your room my Lord." Delia said.

"That would be wonderful." I told her. We followed her out of the kitchen, back down a hall leading toward to front of the house and then up a small stair case that led to the upper floor and then down another hall to the end where a polished cherry door barred the entrance to a grand common room, with a few doors spaced around the room, each presumably a small sleeping area. I took the one on the far right wall, Mica went to the one almost directly across from the door, and Kai walked over to the door on the far left wall and went through.

Mica and I were just about ready to enter our individual

rooms, Delia having turned to leave us, when Kai popped out of his door a second later and called "Delia, this bed is missing some sheets, and, a um, a ah, blanket." I glared at him openly, I knew and he knew and I'm sure Mica knew that there was a blanket and a sheet on his bed just as there was one on mine and Mica's and probably on the beds in all the remaining rooms as well.

Delia was shocked that the room had not been tended to after its last use. "I'll bring them right up." She said hurriedly and ran downstairs again.

"You're incredible." Mica told him.

"I know right?" Kai said back.

"You're a man-whore. You know that?" I told him, half joking.

"Slut." Mica corrected me. "He's a man-*slut*. Whores get paid."

"I seem to be missing how that is a bad thing." Kai said to me.

"Hopeless." I said.

"He'll learn," Mica sighed. "Eventually."

We both turned in unison and closed our doors, leaving Kai to wait for his bed sheets. I wondered if he'd had the sense to hide the ones that were on the bed. I hoped he didn't and she would catch him and beat the crap out of him.

I tried to put Kai and his shenanigans out of my mind as I stripped down to nearly nothing. I turned the lock on the door, and lay on top of the covers wishing there was a window in the room to let in some fresh air. I heard a light knocking and the sound of a door opening and closing as Delia returned with Kai's sheet and blanket that was imperative to have in the ridiculous heat of these little dorm-like rooms. After tossing and turning and rolling around on the bed I managed to fall asleep.

I was jolted from sleep by a scream from across the commons in Kai's room. I fumbled on the floor for my pants and tore open the door. The common area was dark, and Kai's door was open. *What the hell is going on in there!* I asked.

Assassins, it would seem. He told me, a lot calmer than he should have been.

Mica! Get up, now! I yelled in his sleeping head, though how he slept through that scream is another matter.

What's going on? Is something wrong? Mica asked.

No, I'm waking you up in the middle of the night for shits and giggles! I said sarcastically. *Get the fuck up!*

I bent down into a crouching stance, and worked my way across the room toward Kai's door. As I got closer, I could hear Kai talking, but couldn't see him. I counted four figures silhouetted in the room, two just outside the door, one inside holding on to Delia and manipulating her hands into cords that glowed slightly behind her back.

"Let her go, and you can do what you will with me." He told them, his voice calm. "She has nothing to do with anything, she's just a girl."

"Ssshuuut Up!" Came a hissing voice, punctuated by a soft thud, and a grunt, as a fist landed a blow to Kai's gut.

"What do you want with me?" Kai asked, I could hear a twinge of fear in his voice. "Why are you doing this."

"I ssaid," the hissing voice again. "Sssshut up!" There was another, louder thud, followed by the sound of Kai's head

158

hitting the wall.

I stood there, a few feet away from the door, motionless, taking everything in. *What's going on in there? Where are the assassins standing?* I sent the thought to Kai, trying to formulate some kind of rescue strategy.

As I was waiting for Kai's response, I felt a hand on my shoulder and I jumped, spun around on my heal, and rocked back putting my weight on my back leg, and grabbed hold of the wrist that was on my shoulder. I was ready to throw my assailant when I noticed who it was and relaxed. Mica stood there, crouched like I was, though not in a defensive stance. *Next time, just tell me your there, okay?* I asked him.

Sorry! He said in return.

I have five in here, two at the door, one keeping me tied up with these strange ropes that glow, I can't use my majick. Kai answered me just seconds after my encounter with Mica. *There is another standing with Delia. And their leader is in front of me, he's taken a liking to me as a punching bag*

This is not a time for jokes, Kai. I told him.

Says you. He said.

Are you two okay in there? I asked him.

We're not hurt, and they're not assassins, I was wrong. They're working on acquisition and recruitment it would seem. Kai informed us. *If they wanted us dead, I would be dead already. I think they plan to get away with me and use me to get to you two.*

They think we'd actually come get you? Mica commented.

Mica! I yelled at him.

They'd be begging us to take him off their hands. Mica said to me.

Mica, be nice. I told him.

Mica sighed across the link. *What do we do?*

I thought about that for a moment. There are five of them, two of us. If we started tossing majick around, they would sense it and we would have a long, irritating bout on our hands which I would rather avoid. *Don't attack them with majick yet, we still have the element of surprise. They think we're still sleeping no doubt.*

It was at this point that I was wishing Jeoffry were here, so we had at least one more on our side. *I'll get their attention, and when they come out, we'll each take one and quickly, and quietly, subdue them.* I gave the instruction, placing emphasis on the words "quickly" and "quietly" making it clear this had to be fast and quick.

From there, we'll have to improvise as the rest will happen fast. It may turn into us throwing around majick at this point, or Kai being used as leverage. I added one last bit to only Mica. *If it comes down to Kai or Delia, save Kai. Do you understand? Because if Kai dies, then there is no hope of this prophecy being fulfilled.*

I hope you know what you're doing Mattes, if Kai ever found out.... He trailed off.

Do not tell Kai about this, either. As much as I hate secrets, this one is for the best. He wouldn't like it, or understand it. I made myself clear to Mica, and directed him to the other side of the door across from me.

I grabbed a small stone from my pocket that I found on the ground while we were camped for the night on the trip here. For whatever reason, it had caught my eye and I decided to keep it, it was a pretty rock at the very least. I hefted the stone once, to get a feel for its weight, then lobbed it across the room where it clunked on the wooden wall and then fell with a loud thud to the floor and lay there. There was a sudden stillness inside Kai's room and then the hissing voice was hissing out orders to his companions.

"Go sssee who'ss there." the voice said. My heart skipped a beat, as I watched the two figures in the door step away from their post and start making their way through the common area.

I put my weight on my back leg and stayed low, waiting for one of them to get close enough to me. I could hear his boots, faintly, making contact with the floor with each step. And with each step he was closer to me and I steeled myself, keeping my breathing light and my body immobile.

I saw the dark shape of him pass a foot in front of me and I moved, in one swift motion to be right behind him. He stopped, for one second, and I thought he knew I was there. "There's no one out here, master."

"Are you sssure?" came the hissing reply.

"Yesss I'm sure" the man said under his breath, then

162

louder "Yeah, positive."

"Then get back in here" came that now familiar hissing voice again.

It was then, after their exchange, that I struck, hoping Mica was doing the same. I stood up in one swift motion, extended my left arm over his left shoulder and bent it hard and fast at the elbow, placing my right hand on the back of his neck and pushing his throat into my blow. The edge of my hand landed right in the middle of his neck, collapsing his windpipe before he had a chance to cry for help. I caught his body as it fell and lowered it slowly to the ground.

I looked over and saw Mica struggling with his own body as he got it to the ground without making any noise. *Over here.* I said, motioning to Mica.

We stood just outside Kai's room, one of us on either side of the door. I waited there, hoping he would send another one of his goons out after the other two failed to return, but was taken aback when he spoke next. "Very good Matthiasss Boeing. Very good indeed."

The jig was up, so to speak. He knew we were out here.

"You'll pay, no doubt for killing two of my better warriorss, but I have more warriorss, fear not."

"I told you my friends aren't here. Or are you stupid too?" Kai spoke then, and I wish he hadn't because he paid for his words.

"Ssstop lying to me!" He punctuated each word with a blow. "I know they're there. I can tasste their power on my tongue."

Well shit! I thought to the other two. *Kai, you need to work on your negotiating with bad guys skills.*

"Why don't you come out and sssave me the trouble?" the hissing voice said. "No? Maybe if I gave you ssome insscentive."

Kai screamed then, and I could see him struggling against his bonds and his jailer, both of which held tight.

"Please!" Kai gasped. "Just let the girl go and take me! The others aren't here."

"Liar!" Kai screamed in pain again. "They're sstanding jusst outsside thisss door. I'm no fool child."

"Let them go." I said calmly.

"That would hardly be fair." The hissing bastard spoke again. "Why sshould your demandsss be met, but not mine? Hmmmm?"

"Because I know that if I give myself to you freely, you'll just kill the girl, take us to your asshole, scumbag leader, and he'll kill us for not joining is little group of hellion rogue mages on crack." I told him.

"How dare you?" He said.

"How dare *you!*" I countered. I launched every ounce of my majjick at him, drawing a thread of energy from the crystal in my core into my hands and throwing it. I felt it tug on my core as it slammed into him, washing over him. I commanded it to seep into his body, his soul, then screamed with every fiber of my being "Cadere!"

Blood began to seep from his ears, and eyes, and nose. He fell to the ground, glowing with the excess power seeping from his dying body. Blood spewed from his mouth as he coughed up gobs of blood onto the floor and it puddled around his head, and he lay there, motionless.

A second later the two goons holding Kai and Delia were rushing me. I was framed in the doorway, and I took a few steps back, forcing them to come through the door one at a time and thus changing the odds to two to one, the odds being in our favor. They pulled daggers from their robes as they ran, and the first one came through the door expertly slashing his weapons through the air.

Timing my movement, I struck him with a solid blow to his solar plexus, breathing out as my fist struck that spot and imagining my fist going through his body and out the other side. I stepped into the blow and forced him back, and he doubled over. Mica kicked him in the face from the side, causing him to straighten up and fall backward through the door.

The second assailant leaped over the first, flying through the air with supernatural grace and he landed on top of me, grappling me to the ground where we rolled around for a second. I managed to pin one arm on the ground and Mica was kind enough to stomp on his wrist roughly, grinding his foot hard.

That move distracted me slightly and I felt a blossoming

pain across my bare chest and I could feel the blood dripping down. I caught his other arm as he struck out at my throat, a would be lethal blow, and smashed his face with my fist, landing one solid blow to his nose and grinding my fist hard up, and he lay there motionless, blood seeping somewhat from his nose and around his eyes.

Mica pulled the guy off me and helped me to stand. We made our way into Kai's room, and lit the lamps in there, Mica following right behind me. When the light illuminated the room completely, my jaw dropped, I quickly regained my composure. Suddenly I was laughing insanely, happy to be alive, sure, but nothing beat the sight I saw when the room lit up. Kai was standing where he had been, against the wall that the door was on, which explains why I couldn't see him before, but he was completely nude. His booty call or whatever was slouched against the wall across from the door, arms still bound together wrapped around her knees sobbing.

At least the guys attacking us had let her cover up with a sheet.

"How about you stop laughing and come untie me so I can get dressed." Kai said.

"Okay," I said through my cackles. "Alright, just, raise your arms up a bit, I don't want to touch anything accidentally."

"Whatever." He scoffed, and raised his arms up for me to untie him.

While I was untying the rope that was clearly empowered with some form of Majick or spell, I said softly, "So, I see you got your sheets."

"Jealous?" He asked.

"Oh god no, this has to be the most embarrassing thing ever." I told him. "I much prefer being the observer of this situation rather than the observed."

"I'm sure you do, enjoying the show?" He said. "I know it's a lot to take in, but feel free to take your time."

"That's not what I meant and you know it." I retorted.

"Sure. Just untie me." He said.

"Fine." I said back. Louder, to Mica, I said "Can you untie Kai's er, friend?"

"Uh, yeah." He looked a little uncomfortable about it though. What with the whole her being naked except for a thin sheet thing. But he did it, all the same, and managed to preserve what little modesty she had left.

A few seconds later Jeoffry walked through the common room door, and ran over to the room we were in and glanced at Kai quickly pulling on a pair of pants. He looked at Kai, looked at Delia, and just stood there, eyebrows raised. "Well." He said. "Not everyday the phrase 'Caught with your pants down' is given a whole new meaning."

"I could hug you for that." I said. "But first, where in the hell were you five minutes ago?"

"Please, don't. And Sleeping." He told me.

A second behind him was Logan, who assessed the carnage and blood on the ground, glanced at Kai and Delia, and like Jeoffry raised an eyebrow, but he was kind enough to ignore what was already apparent. "Jeoffry--"

"I know naught of what has transpired here cousin." Jeoffry cut him off. "Perhaps you might inquire of my friends."

Jeoffry looked at me. "Don't look at me." I told him, looking at Kai. "I only know how the dead people got here. Kai has all the juicy details."

Kai blushed a bit, and Logan addressed him directly. "Well, speak up boy. What in the bloody hell happened here?"

Kai stood, silent, for a moment, opened his mouth to speak, closed it, opened it again, and closed it. He was silent a moment longer until at last he started to talk. "I, well, I, I mean we, well what had happened was, we were uh." I struggled to not laugh, and was doing really well, but by the gods and any deities out there I wished I could get this on tape.

"I have a pretty good idea of the activity, Kai. I think we're all very aware of that much." Logan spoke up, putting emphasis on the word "very." "Which is a matter to be dealt with at a later time. For now, I think we are more interested in what transpired during the time leading up to the people being dead on my floor in my house."

"Well, I don't know exactly when or how they came in, I was, um, er, distracted momentarily, but I remember Delia screaming and then all of a sudden I was being dragged—off the bed and being tied up." There was a pause after "dragged" where I knew he was about to say something else but changed his mind.

"Distracted, mhm, I see." Logan commented.

"He kept asking me questions like where we were going, and why, and where Mica and Mattes were at. I kept telling him I was here alone, and that Mica and Mattes were elsewhere but he didn't believe me. And that's pretty much where Mattes comes into the picture."

I told them about the fight and how they all died, a look of horror and shock came over both Jeoffry and Logan as I told them how the one on the bedroom floor had died. "You did this?" Logan asked quietly.

"Yes." I told them.

"I feel badly for those who are your enemies, Matthias." Jeoffry told me.

"I've never seen anything like this before." Logan said. "Are you able to do this again, if you had to?"

"I don't know, I would rather not." I said quietly. "I'm not a killer, my Lord. And I do not wish to kill more in this way, because I may go insane if I have to feel another person die."

"You felt him die?" Mica asked.

"Yes. I gave the spell everything I had, and backed it with a word of power. The majick lingered over his body for some time before he was dead, and I felt him dieing, the most unpleasant feeling." I answered him honestly.

"Mattes, you're bleeding." Mica told me.

"Yeah, the last guy got me with his other arm while I was distracted." I told him.

"Here, let me." Jeoffry came over to me, and placed his hand over the gash running down my chest, and his other hand on my back. I felt a wave a warmth move over my body, and thought I peed myself. When I looked down, my pants were dry and there was no longer a gash across my chest. I wiped the blood away, and saw a thin scar on my chest through the faint smearing of blood beginning to dry.

"Thanks." I told him. "So, what do we do now, call the police or something?"

"I'm pretty sure they don't have police here Matthias." Mica told me.

"Guards, the soldiers, the king, I don't know." I said. "Whoever they call when people try to kill you."

Jeoffry coughed, looked to Logan and said "Logan is the Earl here, and is responsible for attending to such incidents."

"So you'll understand when I tell you that this does not look well on my part." Logan looked a little paler, but didn't show any notion of such in his voice which he kept even. "I'll have to send a runner to your uncle, Jeoff, and inform him of the situation. However, these are clearly agents of the Dark Grail, and it is obvious you boys were only defending yourselves."

"Delia, send my two fastest runners up here please." Logan waved his hands toward the bodies laying there.

"Yes my Lord." She said, looking up at him and clutching the sheet tighter around herself. Her cheeks were still stained from her tears and she was still a little shaken. I'm glad he was sending her, so she could get away from this, she looked very uncomfortable here. I watched as she hurried out the door and heard her feet padding down the hall and disappearing down the stairs.

The runners arrived shortly after Delia disappeared from the room, and Logan directed them to their tasks, one was sent to the capitol with a letter Logan wrote at the common room table while we were waiting for them to arrive. The other was sent to the guards on watch. We sat in silent reflection as we waited for the guards to arrive and carry away the bodies.

When the guards showed up, they bore several stretchers, one for each body and each burden was was hoisted by two guards. The stretchers' occupants were covered with white sheets, which quickly became stained with the still wet blood blossoming from the perimortem wounds. Logan spoke quietly to who appeared to be the superior officer. During their conversation the guard glanced at the three of us sitting around the table, and then quickly back to Logan, wide-eyed.

I watched as the guards and their captain filed out the door and tromped down the hall. I'm not sure at what point, but shortly after it was just the five of us in the room again, a thought occurred to me. I spoke it aloud as I thought it.

"He knew my name." I said softly.

"What was that?" Kai asked.

"He knew my name." I repeated.

"Who knew your name?" Jeoffry inquired.

"The leader of the group that attacked us." I explained. "He said my name a few seconds before I--before I killed him."

"That's right." Kai said. "He did, I heard him."

"I remember that, I didn't think anything of it, but yeah. How could he have known your name?" Mica chimed in.

"They must have been following you around the city last night." Logan said.

"Not just my first name, Logan." I told him. "But my last too. And in my time, the part after our name isn't just a title or my father's name, like it is for you guys, but another name. I'm Matthias Boeing."

"This troubles me." Jeoffry was pacing the room now. "It means they know much more about you than we would like. We have no idea how they know what they do."

"From some sort of divination I would expect." I suggested.

"Maybe." Jeoffry agreed. "Or maybe they have spies rooted more deeply within the Kingdom than we know."

"Either way, we're probably not safe staying anywhere very long." Mica said.

"You're right." Jeoffry agreed. "We should leave at first

light."

"Where do you go from here?" Logan asked.

"I'd rather not say, cousin, lest I be overheard." Jeoffry apparently saw the look on Logan's face and added "Nothing against you, cousin. But until we know more about how the Dark Grail is gathering information on us, we need to be careful of where we speak and of what we say."

"I understand, I should think you boys will be needing what rest you can get before your early departure." Logan told us. "You can have the suite down the hall, it's a bit nicer than this one. And I dare say, much cooler. Had I known it was so warm in here, I would have given you that suite originally."

"Thank you." I told him. "I'm tired, though I'm not sure if I'll be able to sleep."

"Understandable, you've had a rough night." Logan told me. "Though do try, lest you fall asleep in your saddle."

The new rooms were much the same as the old, no bigger, though each room did have a window in it, which suggested this suite, unlike the other, faced an outside wall. I tried to sleep, but couldn't for some time. My mind kept replaying the events of the night. We were lucky to be alive, again. The question still remained though, how much luck do we have left?

I tossed and turned all night, never able to get comfortable for long, and when I did sleep it was plagued with nightmares, but what else was new. My sleep was restless as best, and I woke more tired than I was when I fell asleep.

Jeoffry woke us up in the morning, and we went downstairs. In the dining room we enjoyed a quick breakfast of ripe fruit, bacon, and sausage, and a giant pile of scrambled eggs. I ate quickly and stuffed an apple and an orange into either pocket and we left Logan's home, greeted outside by our horses, which had been sent for a little while ago.

The saddlebags were laden again with freshly restocked provisions. We kicked our horses into a trot and set off, down the streets until we reached the open gate and rode through. A road took us around the city and skirted along the wall and across the flat, rough dirt through the familiar tall grass, off to face my enemies, my destiny.

Hunted

I began to hear water later in the day just before dusk. As the sun was beginning to set we were on the banks of a wide river. We made camp here tonight and built a small fire, the air blowing across the water was cool in the night. Having skipped lunch, I partook ravenously of the meager bread and jerky that I had become accustomed to. It was the only thing light enough to be practical to carry long distances without spoiling.

In the morning we rode along the river, looking for a safe place to cross where the water was shallow and slow. We found a place we could cross easily and walked with the horses to the other side. We'd lost the road the previous night and were now riding over open plains which were beginning to shift, a hill appearing hear and there.

As the day wore on the plains seceded to hills, enormous mountains could be seen peeking over the horizon to the north. We routed our path well around any small towns or villages, to decrease the chance of any word of our location or progress. We were counting on Marqus using a physical network of spies rather than majickal means to gather information about us and our whereabouts.

The hills stretched on forever, off into the horizon. They slowed our pace because the horses couldn't sustain being pushed too hard going up the hills. We hadn't seen any sign of human life for nearly three days since we passed the last village yesterday afternoon. I was beginning to grow weary of the saddle and wanted nothing more than to be back at home, in my bedroom on the second floor of Maerik's house, drawing chalk circles on the floor and meditating with candles.

I longed for Maerik's ruthless teaching methods, longed to be drilled on every minute detail of everything he'd ever taught me. I longed for any reality but the one I existed in now, wondering when the next attack would come. I longed to have a normal life, one that didn't involve my being responsible for the fate of a future I'll never see again, I wanted so desperately to be normal. A single tear leaked from my eye and streaked down my cheek, where it evaporated in the wind whipping my face. As I rode along behind Jeoffry, I wondered why he would come with us, and give up everything he had, to join a mission that was destined to fail.

By the end of the seventh day, we were almost to Ashara, just one, maybe two days out, according to Jeoffry and I began to get that weird feeling of dread and anxiety again. I couldn't understand why, though. I was only two days away from at least one night's reprieve of riding and sleeping on the cold, hard ground. I called to Jeoffry to stop and we slowed our horses, wheeling them around to face each other.

"Do you guys feel that?" I asked.

"I don't feel any differently." Kai informed me. "Just a little tired is all."

"No," I told them. "A sense of dread, and anxiety. I had the same feeling before we arrived in Phlenyl."

"And we were attacked there." Jeoffry started to

understand.

"Yeah." I said.

"Well, one thing is clear, Marqus knows you're powerful. And he is going to do anything he can to prevent you from getting anywhere near him. At least, he doesn't want you around on your own terms." Jeoffry said. "He's going to take every opportunity to attempt to eliminate you as a threat, or convert you."

"He's right, I think." Mica agreed.

"Should we skip Ashara?" I asked.

"We can't." Jeoffry said apologetically. "We're already low on supplies, I've been having to hunt at night because we're out of jerky, and there's only a chunk of bread left. If we don't stop in Ashara, we're not going to have food."

"I guess you're right." I sighed.

"We'll just have to be on guard constantly." Mica said.

"Watch everybody's every move. And never let anyone get too close. Ever." Kai said.

There was a chill running down my spine then, and I

wasn't the only one that noticed. Mica took in a quick breath and gasped "Holy shit!"

"What is that?" Kai asked.

"I don't know, but I really don't like it." I told them.

"Demons." Jeoffry said softly. "We have to move. Now!"

Jeoffry kicked his horse into a hard gallop and I followed him, Mica and Kai right behind me. I glanced back, and saw two black shadowy figures that seemed to be made of black smoke. A dark misty substance evaporating off of them as they moved across the ground with supernatural speed in our direction.

"They're getting closer!" I yelled over the thunder of hooves slamming the ground.

Jeoffry yelled a loud guttural yell and pushed his horse faster. The hooves beat the ground causing grass and clumps of dirt as we ran. The demons, or lesser supernatural beings primarily part of another spirit plane and partly of this physical one, had halved the distance between us, and it was becoming more and more apparent that there was no way we could out run them.

I felt Mica as he entered my core and touched the majick there. I felt him drawing the majick from my core. He added my power to the stream of his and Kai's. I felt him twisting our majick through his words, weaving it into the ward he was casting

"Servatis a pereculum! Servatis a maleficum!" He said loudly, over and over, taking it up as his mantra. Mica wove the majick into the ward so as that it would follow us, and surround us. When I was sure the ward he'd cast was complete and stable, I moved up beside Jeoffry.

"Give me your knife!" I yelled across the space separating us, my voice almost completely drowned out by the sound of pounding hooves.

"What?" He called back to me.

"Your knife! Give it to me, now!" I yelled louder.

He fumbled for only a second at his belt before proffering the blade hilt first across the distance separating us. His arm bobbed around slightly despite his efforts to keep it still. Very carefully I reached out and grabbed the hilt, taking it from his hand.

With the reins with my left hand, the knife in my right. My left wrist pointed to the sky, I held the blade to the tender flesh there and drew it slowly across, wincing but keeping my arm still. I kept my arm pressed to the saddle while making the cut, so I didn't jerk against the knife and cut too deeply.

I yelled for everyone to stop and pulled the horses reins, coming to a skidding halt, the horses rearing up slightly. I jumped from the saddle and landed on the ground and rolled, breaking my unstable fall. As soon as I had my bearings a second later I set to work carving a quick circle in the ground, large enough for just the four of us.

Inside I carved several intricate patterns around a much smaller circle in the center. I never took my eyes off the fast approaching beasts who would force themselves on us or ravage the life from our breath, or worse. When the final mark was in place, and the outer and inner circles hastily anointed with my blood, I said in monotone an invocation to the deity to which I'd aligned myself years ago.

Mother Ekydna,
Boon for boon I pray.
Blood of my life sanctifies this circle.

Open your Astral Gate.

Reclaim the dark ones.
In your name I banish them.
By your will I detest them.
By your grace I am free of them.

The circle glowed with Ekydna's acceptance of my offering, the ancient verses written in the old runes burned themselves into the ground. In the center of the inner circle, a soft ball of light began to form, glowing just above the ground.

As the demons approached us, the ball of light, energy, and spirit at the center began to grow taller, and thinner. The glow strengthening with each of their steps. Soon they were just moments away from breaching our circle when the cylindrical beam of light in the center of the inner circle split open wide. As it split, the gash in my wrist bled harder, and I could feel the strength draining from my body as both blood and majick flowed into the ground and fed the invocation.

The pain in my wrist was intense, and my legs weak, I fell to the ground on my knees. Blood pooled at my knee where it dripped from my fingers as it flowed freely from my wrist. The earth at my feet drank hungrily of my blood. As all this

186

happened, the demons were engulfed in blinding light and drawn toward the split in the very fabric of the barrier separating our plane from the spirit plane.

The second they were through the Astral Gate, the circle stopped glowing, the light went away. I was still kneeling on the ground though, seconds away from keeling over. The blood still flowed unabated from my wrist, and Jeoffry was grabbing for my arm as Mica lay me back on the ground.

Moments before Jeoffry placed his hands on my wrist to heal the bleeding gash in my wrist Kai tackled him roughly to the ground. "What in the hell are you doing?" I heard him scream.

"Trying to heal his arm before he dies!" Jeoffry exclaimed.

"Jeoffry," Mica said calmly, tearing off his shirt. "If you use majick to heal this wound, Mattes will die."

"Bullshit!" Jeoffry said, struggling against the pin Kai had him in.

I Gasped with pain as Mica tore his shirt and tied the strips very tightly over my wrist. The cut was much deeper and ragged than I had made it. "It's true." I winced as I spoke.

"Mattes, you're a fucktard, by the way, but that's for later." Kai told me.

"I second that." Mica said. To Jeoffry he explained. "Mattes just used blood majick to invoke his allied deity in order to open the Astral Gates and banish the demons through it."

"And because he used blood majick, he made a pact with his deity, a boon for a boon, Jeoffry." Kai told him. "Ekydna helped to banish the demons, and Mattes must fulfill his boon to her by suffering through this."

"So what can we do." Jeoffry asked.

"Shut the hell up so I can think." I said. "Fuck!" I yelled as Mica tugged hard, securing the final strip of cloth.

"We might as well set up camp." Kai got off of Jeoffry and brushed the dirt from his pants. "Mattes is going to need to sleep so he can heal."

"I'll sleep in the saddle." I groaned, trying to stand up.

"Nonsense." Jeoffry said, also standing.

"Fine, but we ride tomorrow." I told them. "We don't have time for this."

"Someone should have thought about that before using blood majick." Mica mumbled.

"Fuck you." I said to him. "I had no choice."

"I thought only dark majicians used blood majick." Jeoffry said, as though he'd just had some epiphany.

"They use the blood from others." Mica explained to him. "Mattes used his own blood, he knew what would happen, and accepted the burden of Ekydna's boon unto himself, and himself alone."

"That's what separates the good from the bad." Kai said. "In my opinion at least. We protect people, even if it means putting ourselves in danger. Evil cares not for others, but seeks only personal gain, and will go to no ends to have it."

It was then for whatever reason that my body decided it was time for me to pass out. I woke to the smell and sound of meat sizzling just before dusk, and rubbed the sleep from my eyes. When I bent my left wrist to rub my eye, I gasped as it throbbed deeply in pain. It was swollen slightly beneath the bandaging.

"Dude, your shirt." I said to Mica.

189

"I know right? All torn and bloody." He said.

"You don't have a spare though." I told him

"If you live, I think I'll be okay without a shirt for a few more days." He told me, offering me a chunk of fried meat, seasoned with the herbs they'd found. "How's your arm?"

I swallowed a too hot chunk of meat, tore off another burning my tongue again, and swallowed it, before I spoke. "Hurts like a bitch."

"Can you move your fingers?" Mica asked me.

I checked, bending each one painfully. "It hurts, but yeah."

"Good." He told me.

"Good that it hurts or good that I can move my fingers." I asked him.

"Both." Mica said back. "You didn't cut any tendons, and well, maybe the pain will teach you a lesson."

"Ass." I took another bite of the meat and swallowed it, only chewing once or twice. Darkness fell as I gorged myself on the various types of game Jeoffry had caught that night. Long after the others had finished eating, I sat back, satiated and content.

Feeling much better now that I'd had something to eat, I relaxed by the fire, waiting for sleep to come to me again.

"How many more times," Kai asked into the darkness permeated only by the soft glow of the crackling fire. "Do you wager we will win out against the bad guys?"

"It's not like we have an option, is it?" Mica said.

"We have to live." I told them softly. "Every time, we have to."

"But will we?" Jeoffry's voice was the last heard that night. We sat there in silence as the fire burned down to a glowing bed of coals. The night air cool and still. The sound of crickets could be heard faintly through the thick veil of night.

Fate

Ashara is a strange port village bordering on being a small city. All the buildings were of sandstone, browns, reds, grays in various shades. The rooftop of every building was covered in lush green grass. Children could be seen playing in the rooftop gardens from the paths through the village. The paths themselves were lined with larger stones, and were almost entirely sand or fine gravel, and sometimes a mix of both.

This village looked more like a gated community than a river port with the lined paths and growing rooftops. Some exotic looking plants flecked the yards, painting swatches of color over the grassy ground. Tall ship masts could be seen peeking over the tops of houses and huts from a respectable

193

distance away. I found myself thinking that this is a place I could enjoy and live out the rest of my life in. It seemed peaceful and serene, near enough to the river to permit the occasional swim during the hotter days of the year. The small humble homes looked extremely welcoming.

"How long?" Found myself wondering aloud.

"The stable master said it would be three days before another ship leaves for Schötre." Jeoffry told me, understanding.. "We're here until then."

Three days to recover and attempt normalcy, after that, a boat to Schötre. In a week we would be learning the prophecy from Cian, and from there to destroy the leader of the Grail. So quickly comes the day that we win or loose. But this is not a game, and loosing means death. I planned to make the most of three days, or at least enjoy not being on the road, sitting in a saddle from dawn to dusk.

Jeoffry managed to get us a room at this bed and breakfast type place, a widow and her handmaid with an extra room to rent. Expecting another trip to the bathhouse, one I've actually been looking forward to after the last couple of days especially, but also because of the long journey we have ahead. I was caught off guard then, when I learned that the homes here all had hot water pumped indoors.

Jeoffry explained that there were hot springs underground here that were fed to the homes through a crafty piece of majick. Unfortunately the tub in the house was what you would expect a normal tub to be, large enough for only one person. We played rock, paper, scissors to decide who got to go first. Mica won, I was second then Kai with Jeoffry dead last.

I took my turn in the tub, letting the hot water soak away the aches and pains and tightness in my joints. When the grime was scrubbed from my hair and skin, I dressed myself, feeling refreshed and decided to wander around the village for a while. The sun was still in the sky for another hour or two as I walked over the sandy path in front of the home where we were staying. The sand moved around my feet as I stepped through it, leaving a trail of footprints behind me as I moved.

I moved in no particular direction but found myself gravitating towards the masts peeking over the rooftops. I moved on, deep in thought, recalling the events that led me to where I am. I went on like that for some time, daydreaming as I walked to wherever my feet were taking me, having no conscious thought of my direction.

I didn't even see the girl until I'd already plowed right into her, mowing her over, and tripping over my victim I fell too. I landed on my stomach, not having time to catch myself or break my fall. I rolled over and sat up, apologizing profusely. "Are you okay? I'm so sorry, I didn't even see you."

"I'm fine. It's my fault, wasn't paying attention." She said back to me.

"You're out late." I observed, noticing for the first time that the sun was gone from the evening sky and dark had descended.

"I couldn't sleep, so I went out for fresh air." She told me, lifting a hand up to me, waiting for me to help her up.

The moonlight illuminated her pale white face, her eyes a shocking bright blue looked up at me. Those eyes were perched atop sculpted cheekbones. Her face was the most beautiful thing in the light of the moon and I was transfixed by it. I saw her eyebrows arch slightly as I stood there, dumbfound, absorbing her image.

"Oh, yes, right, of course." I stumbled for words, and took her hand, pulling her to her feet a little too quickly. She lost her balance and stumbled forward, and I caught her in my arms. Her head came up to my chin and I looked down at her in the moonlight, studying the face that looked up at me.

We stood there for just a moment but it felt like forever. She cleared her throat and I quickly let her go, and stepped back, feeling a little embarrassed. I could feel myself blushing, warmth blossoming on the apples of my cheeks and spreading outward.

"I'm Matthias." I told her, my voice was soft as I spoke. "My friends, they call me Mattes though."

"Kaila." She said back softly. "And am I one of your friends, Matthias?"

"Do you want to be?" I asked her. "My friend, I mean."

"Well that depends, do you plow them over in the dark often?" She giggled then.

"Only the pretty ones." What in the hell was I thinking, I thought to myself as soon as I said it. "I mean no, no I don't ah--"

She raised an eyebrow and gave me this grin that would bring anyone to their knees. "You're awfully forward, aren't you, Matthias."

"Sorry." I said, blushing harder, looking at the ground which was suddenly very, very interesting.

She laughed, and lifted my head up to look at her. "Walk with me, Mattes?"

I smiled at her, "Sure."

We walked for some time, going nowhere, just moving. We didn't talk, I would look beside me at her now and again, and stare at the profile of her face, the soft white glow of her skin in the moonlight captivating me, drawing me in. She would look over, catch me staring at her, and I would blush and look at the ground again, watching my feet sink into the sand with each step.

"It's beautiful." She said, looking out over the river bank where we had come to stand. The harbor was some distance off to the right, and the moon was full and very large in the night sky right over the river, casting a magnificent reflection on the surface of the water which blurred and distorted the image as it moved downstream.

When I answered her, after a moment, I wasn't talking about the moonscape. "Truly." Was my one word reply.

It was her turn to blush, understanding my meaning. I sat in the grass, and looked out over the river, unable to see completely across to the other side. She sat down beside me a moment later, arranging her skirts around her as she sat.

"Mattes?" Kaila asked quietly in the darkness.

"Yes?" Was my soft reply.

"Do you believe in fate?" She asked me after brief silence.

"I think so." I said. "We all have a destiny, some are just more enjoyable than others. What about you?"

"I'm here with you." Was all she said into the silence.

When I looked over, she was laid back on the ground, staring up at the stars, and I lay back too, looking at the stars. Resting my arms at my sides, my hand touched her arm, she was closer to me than I'd realized. When she didn't move, I brushed my hand down her arm, finding her hand and taking it in mine.

We lay there for what felt like a lifetime, her hand in mine. It fit perfectly in my palm, our fingers interlocked. It felt so natural, so perfect, like our hands belonged together. A breeze blew over the river, and tossed her long, curly locks of burgundy hair around, her soft lavender scent wafting under my nose, my nostrils flaring to catch it as it drifted past.

I turned onto my side, and looked down at her, there was a lock of hair laying along side her face and across her neck, and I brushed it back, my fingers brushing her skin slightly in the motion. She stared up at me and me down at her, eyes locked, breathing in rhythm with each other, in perfect rapport.

"What happened to your arm?" She asked after she saw the bandage as I was brushing the hair from her face.

"I got cut." I told her the half-truth.

"Does it hurt?" She asked me quietly.

"like you wouldn't believe, or it did." I explained. "Mostly just aches now."

Of its own accord, my head moved down, closer and closer to her face until my lips were posed just over hers, a breath away, waiting. Waiting for her to come that last little bit, to close that last breath of a gap between our lips. I waited an eternity, but in reality only a few seconds, for her to meet me.

Her lips were soft, and plump against my own. Sparks were almost visible between us, arcing back and forth as the kiss built in a slow crescendo. When we finally broke the kiss, we were both breathing heavily. I lay back down, and could see her chest rising and falling with my own in my peripheral vision.

I took her hand again, and without thinking, spoke softly to the air. "If I profane with my unworthiest hand this holy shrine, the gentle sin is this. My lips, two blushing pilgrims, ready stand to smooth that rough touch with a tender kiss."

"Good pilgrim, you do wrong your hand too much, which mannerly devotion shows in this. For saints have hands that pilgrims' hands do touch, and palm to palm is holy palmers' kiss." Softly the words were whispered back to me.

"You know Shakespeare?" I asked her, surprised.

"I know naught of him, you recited Bjork just then, did you not?" She asked me.

"Yeah, of course." I said. So, it was true then, Shakespeare did steal Romeo and Juliet from someone else.

"It's a beautiful story." She told me.

"Tragic." I said.

"Beautifully so." She told me. And I couldn't help then, but wonder if we should meet the same ends. She wouldn't follow me into death, I hoped, but my own end could be very, very near.

"We should probably get back." I told her.

"Is something wrong?" She asked, sounding a little hurt.

"No, everything is perfect, absolutely perfect." I said to her, kissing her forehead softly. "I just thought you might want to sleep, it is late."

"Hush." She scooted over closer to me, and lay her head on my shoulder. I pulled her closer to me, not wanting to be any further apart than was necessary. We lay there on the ground for a very long time. My eyes began to drift down, and I opened them again, fighting the sleep. I could hear Kaila's soft, sleepy breaths on my chest, and eventually relaxed into the soft bed of grass, more comfortable on the ground now than any other night. Whether it was because she was there with me, or this was uncommonly soft dirt has yet to be discerned.

I lay my head against hers and fell asleep. For the first time since we left the clearing and woke up at Ephraim's I slept well. Her body fit perfectly against mine, like we were made to fit together. Nothing ever felt so right, so perfect before. I slept a sound sleep, and dreamed only of her, and that perfect face lit by the moon.

I could feel the morning sun on my face, warm and gentle. Kaila was snuggled in close to me, head on my chest and her arm wrapped around me. I could feel her breathing on my neck, she stirred once, and slept on.

Stalker. I silently told Kai, who I knew was sitting in the grass about five feet behind us without opening my eyes to see him.

We were worried, you never came home last night. He told me.

Well I'm fine, I can take care of myself, Kai. I shot back.

Well, that's pretty obvious. Kai showed me exactly what he was seeing: Kaila and I sprawled on the ground, her skirts flowing around her, her hair in less than perfect condition, all the while she was draped over top of me, face nearly buried in my neck. *I didn't know you had it in you.*

Had it in me? I asked, not understanding him, then it dawned on me exactly what he had meant by that. *This is not what it looks like Kai. We talked, that's all.*

You talked? Really? Nothing else? Kai seemed intrigued, or disbelieving.

Yes really. Well, we may have kissed, but that's all. I told Kai.

Wow. A kiss. Serious business. Kai teased.

Why in the hell am I telling you this? I wondered. *Get the hell out of here, Kai.*

Fine. He said, and sulked off, back the way he came.

Kaila yawned about twenty minutes later, and stretched, extending her arms and legs. "You're here." She whispered, her voice groggy.

"Thank God." I said back, kissing her forehead.

Her smile reached the eyes that stared into my own. It is said that your eyes are portals to the soul, and what I saw in those eyes was so beautiful, so pure, so humbling, so innocent, I felt I could loose myself in them for a lifetime. I wanted just then, to do just that. To loose myself in those eyes and forget everything, forget about Cian and the Prophecy and the Dark Grail and everything else but staying lost.

"What are you thinking about?" She asked me, drawing my attention from my thoughts.

"Your eyes." I whispered to her. "They're beautiful."

She blushed, and said "Thank you."

"We should get you home." I told her.

"I have a room near where we ran into each other last night." She told me.

"You don't live here?" I asked her.

"No, I'm from Trent, in the south. I'm on my way to Schötre." Kaila explained, a sadness in her voice.

"I'm going to Schötre too." I told her. "In hopes of

contacting an old friend."

"What then?" She asked. "Do we part ways?"

"Never!" I said passionately. "We'll always be together."

"You're so sure." She said, disbelieving.

"Because I am." I reassured her. "I shall never leave you."

"Promise?" She asked, hopefully.

"Promise." I said, standing and helping her up with me. "Let's walk."

We walked together back across the grass and the sand paths that were intricately woven through the small town. Back along the way we had come, I didn't recognize any of the scenery from the darkness last night. All the same we made our way back to where I mowed her over last night and stopped.

"My friends are probably worried." I told her.

"Why should they worry for you?" She asked me.

"Let's say we haven't had the safest journey." I told her. "Danger lurks in every shadow and behind each corner, waiting to catch me unaware. I suppose you should know that

206

before we go any further."

"Is life worth living without danger?" She spoke softly. "Is fear worth losing you?"

I looked right into her eyes, and saw a strength and fearlessness there, and spoke back to her in the soft tone she'd used. "Questions only you may answer. Know that I would never forgive myself if you were hurt–or worse."

"I can take care of myself, Mattes." She said. "Do not worry over me like a milk maid."

"I'll try." I joked. "Will you have dinner with us later?"

"There is a small kitchen near the center of town," she explained. "You can meet me there just before sunset."

"Great." I said, and started to take a few steps backward. She turned and walked away, down an adjacent path and then turning out of sight down another. I turned and wandered back along the sand path and turning down another corner I recognized the place where we had gotten a room the night before.

My hand hesitated over the door knob, hovering there, unsure. Kai had already caught me laying on the riverbank with a girl I'd met only hours prior and only by mere clumsiness. Granted Kai was caught nude with a maid, but somehow sleeping twined on a bank seems so much more intimate.

Against my better judgment, I pushed down on the latch and the door swung open gently. I stepped inside and latched the door behind me, making my way to our room. I paused briefly at the door and took a breath, and as I entered all three of them looked at me, they had clearly just stopped talking.

"Hey." Jeoffry said to me as I came through the door.

"Hey." I said.

"Kai told us he found you with a girl." Jeoffry said.

"Yeah. What about it?" I asked him.

"Do you love her?" He asked me.

"I don't know, I think I do." I answered.

"And when we leave here?" He asked.

"She's coming with us." I told him.

"Mattes!" Mica yelled.

"You can't bring her, Marqus sends assassins like nobody's business." Jeoffry explained. "She could be hurt."

"She was already on her way, she's waiting for the boat like we are." I told them.

"What in the hell are we going to do with you Mattes?" Kai asked me.

"Look." I told them. "I can take care of myself."

"Yeah, but can you protect her too?" Jeoffry asked me. "Can you be with her every moment, of every day, from now until the time Marqus dies?"

They had a point, she was a weakness. If she were caught she could be used against me. I couldn't think about that now, though. "Don't you think I know all of this? I can't control what I feel, and I don't wield fate's reigns."

"Just be careful Mattes." Jeoffry told me.

"I know." I said. "Do you guys want to meet her later tonight for dinner?"

"We have to eat, and we might as well meet this girl you're courting." Jeoffry said. "In the meantime, we need to sell the horses, we won't be needing them."

"Where does one go to sell his horse?" I asked inquisitively.

"Often, the stable master will take them off your hands, but when I talked to him yesterday, he was only selling horses at the time." He told me. "We might try the others in town. With some luck we'll have the horses taken care of in time for dinner."

We did have them taken care of before dinner, only just, and only by chance. Apparently, the horses were too worn to be useful for anything but plowing fields. That would have been fine, if someone would have just told us from the beginning. Instead, stable masters were turning us away left and right with a bit of lip-service and gusts of hot air

We ran around all day, until a nicer older man finally told us the truth and ended the torment and irritation. "Tah tell yah da truth maty, dese horse, day ain' good fur much mer den plowin' meh field." He had such a terrible accent that I could hardly understand him. When his lips moved it was almost like you had taken a Scottish sailor, raised him in Ireland, who had also spent a large portion of his life in London or something. The culmination off the mixture of sound his voice made was so harsh. The entirety was made worse yet by his apparent age, which made his voice harsher still, in that way old peoples' voices get that weird raspy lilt or pitch to them.

We ended up selling the horses to him, Jeoffry worked out the details. Most of the other stables in the town sold to merchants and the the shipyards and shipping companies as there were few farmers in the area. This guy dealt with the few farmers in the area, apparently managing a small farm himself. I couldn't imagine much of anything growing in this sandy soil, maybe better described as dirty sand, as there was much more sand than dirt.

It was nearly dusk when the horses were finally completely squared away. We stopped back at the house where we were renting a room, and took baths and changed clothes. I had originally thought we were going to have to grab some fresh clothes when we got settled in, because everything we'd brought with us was completely threadbare. All of my pants had holes worn through, the hems of the legs falling apart, strips of cloth hanging off them. My shirts were torn and little more than rags. Thankfully, the lady who owned the house, was like any other grandmother. She cooed over us and clucked like a mother hen when the hand maid presented her to us. Apparently, she had clothes from sons, and grandsons that fit us quite well stored in a little alcove in the loft at the top of the house.

Jeoffry tried to explain that we could just grab some stuff at the market down by the docks later, but she insisted. I was happy to have clean clothes that weren't bloody and full of holes. The fact that I didn't have to go shopping made everything that much better.

Eager to meet Kaila at the kitchen, and pretty hungry too, I rushed to the tub and quickly scrubbed my hair and washed the sweat and dirt from the hot windy day from my skin. I paced back and forth in our room as I waited for the other three to finish and dress. I practically ran down the paths through town that lead to a squat little building with a couple chimneys pouring smoke from their spouts.

The sun had set and with it the heat waned from the air. The moon waxed into the sky, chasing away the sunset as darkness descended, the soft shadows of night beginning to replace those of the hot daytime sun. Inside were a myriad of tables and chairs, we chose a table in the corner large enough for six people and sat down, not seeing Kaila yet. After about five minutes, we were still waiting, but the those five minutes felt like an hour. The sun was still casting a glow just above the horizon.

"It's okay Mattes, you can tell us." Mica cooed. "You're the only one who can see her, aren't you?"

My jaw dropped then, and my eyes popped, but not because of what Mica had said, but because Kaila just stepped up behind him, and she looked more beautiful in the soft glow of the candle and fire light than she had the night before. Her lace and satin dress was magnificent, a little dated, but still brilliant.

She tapped Mica on the shoulder with a long, pale polished finger and asked "Is this seat taken?"

Mica looked up at her, a stupid look on his face, and she raised an eyebrow and he stuttered around for a few seconds before managing to get "Uh, no, uh, here." out of his lips then standing up and pulling the chair out for her. Everyone was laughing at him as she sat down beside me. Mica took the last open seat at the table beside Kai right across from me.

213

Mica blushed a bit, pink seeping up his neck and creeping over his cheeks as he sat down. When the laughing and giggling had mostly subsided Jeoffry addressed Kaila. "I'm Jeoffry." He lowered his head to her, and went on. "Mattes has told us absolutely nothing of you."

"Nor I you." She said glancing sidelong at me, and elbowing me playfully. I felt something hard brush against me, but thought nothing of it. "I'm Kaila, gentlemen." She kinda ducked in her chair in a sort of impromptu sitting curtsey.

"From where do you hail?" Jeoffry asked.

"Trent, in the south." She told him.

"You're awfully far from home." He said. "Why do you venture so far north? You'll forgive my curiosity of course, won't you?"

"Of course." She said. "I'm a woman of business and my wiles bring me here."

"I see." He commented.

We chattered on idly as the room slowly filled with people who were either traveling, didn't feel like cooking, or sailors. The predominant variety of soup kitchen pilgrims were sailors, enjoying the rare trip and meal ashore. When the room was nearly full staff began to move around the room with bowls, handing them out amongst the crowd. When they got to our table, Jeoffry tossed a few gold pieces into a pot carried by another directly behind the man with the stack of bowls.

When at last everyone had a bowl, the wait staff returned with large pots suspended between two people on a small pole, a third dipping soup into each bowl. Another group of people were moving around the room handing out chunks of freshly baked bread, a large variety available. There was still small wisps of steam escaping into the air as chunks of bread were torn from the massive loafs and passed out.

I ended up taking a yeasty chunk of warm rye, a nice crispy crust around the edge. The rye seeds were always a surprising burst of flavor when I bit into them. The bread coupled with the richness of the potato stew were perfect compliments. We nursed the hot soup, eating it with the warm bread. I burned my tongue with the first bite, trying to devour a spoonful without thinking.

We laughed and joked through the meal, Jeoffry told a few jokes that I pretended to get but had no idea as to the meaning. Kaila enjoyed them, though she was the only one familiar with the time period. We all got on quite well, I had half expected Kai and Mica to be unable to take this seriously and do nothing but make jokes at my own or Kaila's expense all night.

I drained the last drop of creamy soup from my bowl and pushed it back, nibbling on my bread. A couple others in the room, along with Kaila and Jeoffry, were still eating. Kaila suddenly stiffened, she dropped her spoon and it fell, hitting the edge of the bowl and flopping onto the table. Her back straightened and her eyes rolled up to the ceiling.

"Kaila?" I said in a hushed yell, nudging her a bit. "Kaila? Are you okay? Kaila!"

A few seconds later she was fine again, but a fine bead of sweat gleaned on her forehead. "We have to go, quickly!"

"What do you mean? Where do we have to go?" I asked her, worried.

"That woman you're staying with, she's in trouble." She told me.

We all stood up, and it was Jeoffry who asked "What kind

of trouble?"

"I don't know, I couldn't see their faces." She explained. "I only saw them chasing her."

"Wait," Kai said, stopping. "You saw them? How? When?"

"I'll explain later." She said in a loud whisper, we were beginning to attract attention from the other people in the room. "We have to go, now!"

We hurried out the door and down the sand paths, breaking into a run as soon as we were off the steps to the kitchen. Sand flew in our wake as we ran, I had half hoped Kaila would fall behind, I didn't want her anywhere she could get hurt, but she was right beside me the whole way. We glanced at each other, and I could see the determination in her eyes and I knew she was coming, and I could never dissuade her.

As we got closer to the house I was beginning to feel a sense of wrongness in the air, as sense that something was not right. The only thing that I knew for certain was this was yet another attempt by Marqus to destroy us.

"No!" Came the frail voice of Maud, the woman who

owned the house. We were less than fifty yards away when we heard her scream. "Please, no! Please, stop."

I could feel the blood rushing through my veins, pounding in my ears. My feet pounded the sand, I ran faster and faster, wanting to get there before it was too late. Before she was dead. When I got to the door, it was ripped from the hinges, the hand maid lay in a bloody and broken heap just inside, blood pooling around her body, and smeared and splattered over the walls.

I jumped over the body and continued onward closer to the pleas and screams. Five figures stood in the dining room, the heavy table that once sat in the center smashed into pieces in the corner, the candelabra that had stood in its center mottled and bent in the heap, glass from the chandelier cascaded over the floor in the center of the room, glinting and winking in the moon light from the window.

Their backs were to me when I stopped in the door, they formed a semi-circle around Maud, cutting into her flesh with a bloodied knife. Maud's eyes met mine, tears and pain and horror and fear filled them to the brim and they overflowed, washing over me. Her lips parted in a whimper, a feeble plea

218

whispered hoarsely to me, before the black robed figure turned his head to see me in the door. As soon as he saw me he murdered Maud, slicing the blade across her throat and letting her crumple onto the floor, what blood remained in her veins now pooling on the floor as it seeped from the deep gash..

All five of the figures were facing me now, ten eyes glowing at me from under their deep cowls. They emanated a dark light, I can't explain it, but the closest definition is the culmination of darkness and evil with a black light. Chills ran down my spine as they moved slowly toward me, one step at a time, in no hurry.

I took a step back out of fear and horror, and another step before I turned and ran right into Jeoffry as the rest of the group caught up to me. "Turn around, go, go!."

We ran back out of the house onto the front lawn. "Mattes, what happened, is Maud okay?" Jeoffry asked me.

"No." I said sadly, having seen her last moments. "And neither are we as soon as whatever those things are get to us."

"What the hell?" Mica said as the first of the robed things stepped from the door and continued advancing toward us.

"Kaila, go somewhere safe." I said behind me.

"No." Was all she said in response.

"Please, Kaila." I begged her.

"Don't worry about me." She told me.

"Kaila, I need you to leave, for me." I told her, and then quietly, sincerely I continued. "I love you, and if you love me, you'll run and hide."

"Mattes--" She said softly. "Don't make me leave you."

"Please." I begged.

I heard the rustling of her dresses and the padding of her feet as she turned and ran back in the direction we came. The hooded figures were only ten feet away now and closing on us. The way they marched perilously closer to us scared me to death. I was still drawing a blank when trying to figure out what these things were.

"I'll take the two on the end, you guys can have the other three." I said, crouching into a stance I was familiar with.

"You're not superman Matthias." Mica told me, crouching as well.

"Yeah, well, neither are you, I've just spent more time on the mats." I said back, taking a deep, calming breath through my mouth. I let the air fill my lungs from the bottom, relaxing my abdomen as the air slowly flowed through my lips. The creatures were marching ominously forward and I began to exhale slowly through my nose, tightening my core in anticipation.

My heart beat heavily in my ears, the loud whooshing sounds filling my head. When the last of the air was released, our enemies were only a few feet a way, I could step forward and poke them. I took one quick breath from my nose and smelled fear and terror in the air. I saw the other three leap and grapple in my peripheral vision moments before my two targets were an arm's length away.

Time slowed down, and my vision narrowed to just those two black clad figures, my mouth went dry and my nostrils flared as I struck out at the solar plexus of the one on the right, stepping into the blow and under the arm that had swung out to me, my body instinctively pivoting on its heal and grabbing his arm as the force of my blow carried him back. I felt, more than heard, his shoulder being wrenched from its socket as I drew him over my shoulder and onto the ground in front of me.

My heart raced faster and sweat broke on my face, running into my eyes and stinging them. Neither of my assailants seemed be be affected by the injuries they were sustaining. The one with the dislocated shoulder rose off the ground only moments after I put him there, catching me off guard when he tackled me to the ground and began to throw fiendish, mindless blows at my head, anything to kill me.

He caught me on my cheek before I managed to throw him off of me and leap off the ground. When I was standing again, one of the monsters again laying on the ground the other was not in my line of sight. I crouched down into a fighting stance, grounding myself, steeling myself.

A sharp pain erupted on my right side, I heard a loud crack. I tried to block the pain of the broken rib as I fought off the other thing which was nowhere to be seen moments before. I dodged and ducked blows, landing what I could, but my body was beginning to tire, and every part of me was beginning a dull throb, canceled slightly by endorphins and adrenaline.

The other one was off the ground now and advancing toward me, and I had yet to dispatch my current assailant. Gaps were beginning to open up in my defensive maneuvers, I was getting slower, more tired. These things were tireless, and unable to be injured it seemed. I tried to charge my hands and body with energy, but it was as effective as tasering a rock.

I dispatched the ones I was currently grappling with using a deft hard kick to its face, spinning on the ball of my left foot and striking with my heal as I came around, I directed the blow down slightly and he fell. The other was almost on top of me as the one closest to me hit the ground and I continued my momentum and brought my foot right into the side of his right knee, and he fell kneeling, I was breathing more heavily now, trying to catch my breath.

"We'll you're alive." A voice said behind me.

"I know you're not talking to me." I yelled back, not looking away from my targets. The one without the shattered knee was trying to sit up and I kicked him hard enough to

223

completely destroy the vertebrae in his neck, which should theoretically make him dead. This guy didn't seem to understand that he should be dead though, as evidenced by bone poking through his neck, the skin jutting out at odd angles.

"So, you figured out how to kill them yet?" I recognized Kai's voice.

"Breaking their neck doesn't work." I remarked.

"Why do I not find that surprising?" Mica asked.

"Why in fuck are you asking me?" I said. "We'll figure out your sadistic thought patterns after these things are gone."

The one with the broken neck tried to get up again. The other one kept falling back down as it unsuccessfully tried to hop toward me, but lost it's balance mid-way. It was now crawling, using its one good leg and its arms to edge itself forward, inching his way closer to me.

The other was standing, neck jutting, and moving toward me. I was beginning to feel really pissed. I was no longer fighting constantly, so some of the adrenaline had subsided, and now I was irritated and needed to lay down. I steeled myself for what I knew was going to hurt and kicked him in the left leg with every piece of frustration I had. Every last scrap of anger and grief and hate was packed behind that kick and the blow connected as squarely as I could have hoped.

The crack was loud, wet, and sick sounding and the bone splintered and shattered, pieces popping out of the skin. I followed the kick to his knee with another hard blow to his chest tossing him backward, unable to stand.

"Oh shit!" I heard Kai yell. "Oh shit, oh shit, oh shit!"

"What the hell Kai?" I asked him.

"Caocladh." He said. "They're fucking Caocladh."

"What in the hell are Cao-whatevers?" I asked him.

"They're soulless shells." He said. "They'll keep coming until they can't move, or they're destroyed."

"And how are they destroyed?" I asked.

"Fire, then their ashes are spread in running fresh water." He answered.

"Wait, how in the hell do you know this?" Mica yelled. "You

don't normally have random information stashed in your brain."

"What, I can't be intelligent sometimes?" Kai asked him.

"Well, it's just not characteristic of you is all." Mica said.

"Right, so now I'm an idiot?" Kai asked, feeling alienated.

"Jeoffry, if either of them say anything else not related to making these things charcoal, hit them." I said, risking a glance over my shoulder at Jeoffry who gave me a little tilt of his head, letting me know he knew I was serious and that he would do it.

"Let's move them into a pile over there before they crawl off or do something bad." Jeoffry said, pointing to a spot on the edge of the wispy lawn.

"Be careful though, they're still very much alive, if you will. They're still dangerous." I called over to them.

"Duly noted, Mattes." Mica said.

I walked over to one of the two things laying on the ground, and grabbed it's left ankle and began to drag it to where Jeoffry had pointed. There was a stab of pain in me left side, and I felt the leg I was holding onto twisting and jerking. I gasped and caught the other leg when he brought it back around to strike again and held fast.

"Are you okay?" I heard someone call.

"Yeah." I groaned. "Fine. I'll be fine. Let's just get this over with.

The once still darkness was becoming less still, less silent. I could hear people moving around their homes, could see window treatments being moved, exposing the soft glow of a candle stick just behind the glass. "You guys, we should probably pick up the pace, people are starting to notice." I said to them as quietly as I could and still be heard.

Through all this, my arm never bothered me. While dragging the thing to the burn pile however, the scab on my left arm split painfully. I could feel the bandage becoming wet with the blood spilling from the crack.

"Right." Mica said from behind me. I jumped a bit, I didn't hear him coming. "Well, right here is good enough." He heaved the body he had in tow onto a spot just in front of us and I tossed mine right on top.

"Would you like the honors?" I asked him.

"Let's just do it together, it will go faster." He said.

"Okay then." I reached down into my core and connected with the energy there, and called up my majick, spinning the different flavors into a raging inferno. We expelled the power simultaneously and the two bodies caught fire, acrid smoke rising from the burning flesh.

Jeoffry was there, a moment later, heaving a load of fresh fuel onto the fire. I Passed Kai as I went back for the last Caocladh. With all five of the things burning, and people now out in the streets looking on, I was unsure of what to do. Kaila was out there somewhere, hiding.

I sat down on the ground, wincing in pain the whole way, while we waited to collect the ashes. "What happened to you Mattes?" Jeoffry inquired when he heard me trying to sit on the ground.

"It's nothing." I said. "Probably just a bruised rib."

"Let me see." Jeoffry said. "It could be worse."

"It's fine." I insisted.

228

"Well then, if its fine, then it won't make a difference if I take a look, will it?" Jeoffry asked.

"Mattes?" Mica made my name a question.

"Yes?" I answered.

"Will you just shut the hell up and let him take a look at you?" Mica sounded irritated, so I pulled my shirt from my breeches and showed Jeoffry what was sure to be a nasty green purple and black bruise spreading along my ribs.

He poked around with a couple fingers, feeling the area, and the next time he touched my rib cage, I gasped as pain shot through me and knocked his hand away. My sudden movement did nothing for the pain, but it was a reflex.

"Well?" I raised my eyebrows.

"You have at least two broken ribs." Jeoffry lowered his eyes.

"Of course I do." I sighed. "Well, you can heal it can't you, like you did back at your cousin's?"

"That was flesh wound, bones are much more complicated and difficult." He explained.

229

"But you can try can't you?" I looked at him.

"You didn't even want me to look at this a minute a go." Jeoffry said. "Why the change of heart?"

"Because I can't fight with a broken rib." I told him.

"I'll try, but it won't feel good, and at best I can only speed up the process, give you a week's worth of healing at most. You'll still have to be careful." He placed his hand over my ribs, and at first there was a warmness spreading out from his hand, soothing the wound. But that lasted for only a second before the bones began to realign themselves, and grow back together. The pain was indescribable, I clenched my fists and squeezed my jaw closed, not wanting to vocalize my pain any more than the loud winces and groans.

The pain intensified threefold before it ended and Jeoffry took back his hand and I fell back, gasping on the ground. My vision blurred momentarily and when it returned to normal I could see Kaila running up, dodging through the people who had come out to watch the aftermath of the fight.

Kaila was crying when she fell to her knees beside me, tears streaking down those soft, beautiful cheeks. "You're

230

hurt." She said.

I reached up and brushed a strand of hair from her face and brushed a tear from her cheek. "I'm fine."

"Don't lie to me, Mattes, I can see that you're hurt." She said, choking back more tears. "How bad?"

"Just a couple broken ribs, Jeoffry fixed me up a bit though." I told her. "I'll be fine, I promise."

"You'd just better be." She said, trying to smile. I stared into her glistening eyes and rose up on my arms a bit, pulling her face down to mine gently, and kissed her softly. I hated to see her upset, it hurt me so deeply to see her like this.

"Listen to me." I whispered when we parted. "I'm going to be fine, don't worry about me, I've felt worse." I thought back to the time just before I managed to wake up at Jeoffry's back in Michval.

The bodies burned for a little over an our, their own blood seemed to act like a catalyst, speeding up the burning process. Even while being barbequed, the Caocladh refused to take it laying down and would attempt to move or thrash even as their limbs crumbled to ash. As the flames died the small crowd began to disperse, no doubt each and every one of them dreaming up some piece of mighty gossip to share with their neighbors over coffee or tea the following day.

Jeoffry and the others collected every last scrap of ash in a pot they found in the old lady's kitchen and carried it down to the river where they cast the ashes into the running water. I wanted to go with them, but Kaila insisted I shouldn't be running around and that I needed rest, and the others were in agreement.

Kaila and I walked to the nearest tavern and got some coffee while we waited for the others to come back. We found a table in the corner and sat together on the bench, our coffee all but ignored as it got cold. We sat there, holding each other for a solid hour before the door swung open and Mica popped through, followed by Jeoffry with Kai in Tow.

The three of them sat down across from Kaila and I. I looked at Kai and raised my eyebrows in a question. "So, O Wise One, care to explain what Caocladh are?"

Kai scowled severely at me for a few seconds before he tried to answer. "You know the phrase, 'Sell your soul to the Devil?' Right?"

"Of course, who doesn't?" I asked, but then I noticed the look on Jeoffry's face which was mirrored on Kaila's and said "You two don't count."

"Why not?" Kaila asked indignant.

"It's complicated." I told her. "You probably wouldn't believe me anyway."

"Try me." She said.

"Not right now, later." I said, then to Kai; "What of it?"

"Well, it's a bit like that, except Marqus, or whoever sent them, is the devil." Kai explained.

"You don't mean...." I trailed off.

"I do." Kai went on. "The soul is our essence, our very being, the reason we love and hate and even feel pain. When you detach the soul from the body you're left with little more than a mindless shell that doesn't feel pain, love, fear, or hate. All they know is what they were created for."

"Who would do such a thing?" Kaila said, disgust and fear on her face and laced through her voice.

"Only the most evil and sinister people. The heartless

233

scum of the world." Jeoffry said.

"Who would be willing to submit to such a fate?" Mica asked.

"No one said they had to be willing." Jeoffry said, his voice sad.

"So we just destroyed five innocent men." My voice was weak.

"There's no helping them, no reversing the process, they had to be destroyed." Kai, I could tell, shared my pain. "Their souls are trapped here until the body is destroyed, a soul and a body can not fully be parted, one existence is always tied to the other. We did them a favor, Mattes, even if they were innocent men, we set their souls free."

"Marqus has to die for this, even more than before." I said, anger filling me. "It's one thing to try and kill us, we are his enemy after all, but using innocents as a pawn to meet those ends, that is unforgivable."

"I agree." Mica said to me and everyone else.

We sat in silence for a while, when a gruff man came to offer Kai and the others something to drink, I got a warm up on my coffee, which I started to nurse. I let my thoughts wander to the room for a moment, wanting to take my mind away from the horrors of a fate I didn't ask for, and everything I feared to come, as well as all that has come to pass.

It was a plain room, with plain walnut tables and benches, their surfaces worn from the hundreds of patrons that sat there before us, the edges rounded and gouged in some places. The floor was of knotty pine and cedar paneled the walls. The cedar panels were all aged, except for a small group near the door that appeared decidedly newer. Replaced after a late night brawl perhaps?

"I hesitated." I said quietly, my lips moving of their own volition. Perhaps I was trying to distract myself from more than just fear and my destiny.

"What do you mean, Mattes?" Kaila asked, hugging me.

"I ran ahead of you guys, and she was there, propped against the wall." I could barely hear myself as I spoke, my voice was quiet, hurt, ashamed. "She looked right at me, begging with her eyes for me to save her, and I hesitated, when they saw me, they, they killed her. I should have done something."

"What Matthias, what could you have done?" Kai looked right at me, staring at the top of my head as I studied the grain of the wood on the table. "They're impervious to majick, Mattes, you couldn't have done anything without getting yourself killed."

"Better me than her. She didn't deserve that."

"They would have just killed her the second you were dead. Don't lie to yourself Mattes." Kai told me what I already knew, but that didn't change anything, I just sat there.

"If you die, Mattes, then what?" Mica asked me. "What becomes of our future, what becomes of now, who then will destroy Marqus?"

"But how many more have to die before Marqus meets Death and his undoing? How many more?" I may have said the last part a little more loudly than what I should have, before I heard my chair falling to the floor as I stood, and left.

Ships, Men and Sabotage

The air was cool against my skin, my hair was getting longer, I noticed, as the wind gently tossed it around. I found myself hoping this time had found a need or desire for barbershops or something. My heart had calmed itself and I could no longer hear the beating in my ears. I laughed at nothing and everything quietly to myself.

I thought about running, I wanted to run and to never stop, but there was no escaping Marqus, he's made that clear, as long as he's alive I have no choice but to lay in wait of his next assault, and pray that I can overcome it. We're supposed to be so freaking powerful and yet I constantly feel powerless. Why is it always like that?

I found myself at the edge of a steep bank, the river could be heard gurgling softly down below. I decided I wanted to be closer to the water and climbed down, careful not to bump my arm, sitting on the rocks and sand at the water's edge. I let my hand drag through the water, watching it flow around and between my fingers. Small whirlpools spun off and dissipated back into the current. I let a drop of energy well at the tip of my finger, swirling it in the water creating a small whirlpool that broke the surface of the water enough to hide my reflection.

When the flow of majick stopped, the whirling water dissipated as before back into the current, flowing downstream. "Feel better?" I heard Jeoffry's voice behind me, at the top of the bank.

"Well, that depends." I said.

"Oh?"

"If you're asking about my ribs, my wrist, or the impending doom that follows us wherever we go."

"Well, let's start from the beginning and work our way down the list, shall we?"

"Fine, my ribs hurt like a son of a bitch. The gash on my wrist broke open while I was dragging those things. Oh, and don't forget, we can't go more than a few days without Marqus devising some new way to kill or capture us." I said all this very fast, must more quickly than I normally spoke.

"Mattes, you're in shock." Jeoffry jumped from the top of the cliff to the small beach below. "You're under a lot of stress tonight."

"What fucking else is new?"

"Let me take a look at your arm. I'll wrap again until it scabs back over."

I sighed and extended my arm, without getting up. "I'm an idiot."

"You're not an idiot." I felt Jeoffry's eyes boring into me.

"I dragged Kaila into all of this. I should have been paying attention to where I was going and then she wouldn't be involved at all."

"Do you honestly think you would be better off without Kaila?" Jeoffry said, tugging on the strip of cloth he was trying to tear off his shirt.

"No, but she would be safe." I gritted my teeth as he tied the shirt around my arm, pulling it tightly.

"Sorry." He said.

"For what? Don't be a fool, Jeoffry, I held the knife when I cut me." I told him.

"But you did it to save us."

"All of us, Jeoffry, that includes me too."

"If I could bear it for you, I would."

"Jeoffry, don't say that, words can carry power. This is my burden, and I will bear it as I should."

"So I could then?"

"You won't even think about it, Jeoffry. I told you, it's my burden, my decision. Not yours." I stood and started walking toward the cliff. "Let's get back."

I made my way up the cliff, finding it easier to go up than down, I pulled myself over the top and waited for Jeoffry to catch up. "Pretty bad when the cripple beats you up a cliff." I called down to Jeoffry.

"I was making sure you didn't fall." He called back. He

attached himself to the dirt and rocks and made his way up the cliff face.

"Yeah, right." I said.

I offered my better hand to him when he was at the top and helped him over. "So, now what do we do? We have no place to stay."

"You're just now realizing this?" He asked me.

"Well, no, I'm just now deciding to make it a topic of discussion." I said.

"Okay." He held the last syllable for a breath, making it a question wrought from uncertainty. "Well, before I decided to come searching after your stupid ass, I talked to someone at the kitchen and they happen to have two rooms free."

The way he said the last part had me feeling slightly uncomfortable. And so it was my turn to elongate the last syllable of a single word sentence. "Okay."

He looked at me awkwardly and said, "I thought Kaila and yourself might share a room, and the rest of us the other."

"I'm not like Kai, Jeoffry. I don't have sex with anything

241

with two legs and a pair of boobs." I explained, I didn't want Jeoffry to think Kaila and I would be in the next room doing it like bunnies.

"Oh, no, I didn't think. I mean, of course not." He stammered.

"It's cool, Jeoffry. I just don't want you thinking that I'm like that." I told him.

There was one of those awkward silences, the tension thick enough to cut with a knife. I tried to think of something to say into that silence but was struggling to think of something. I was startled when Jeoffry spoke, breaking the silence. "Right, so, we leave tomorrow. To Schötre at last."

"Yeah." I said. "At last."

"We'll be fine Mattes." Jeoffry assured me.

"How can you know that?" I asked him. "Do you really believe it? Honestly?"

He was quiet during the walk back, thinking perhaps about what I'd said or maybe of something entirely different. Soon enough we were back at the kitchen, it was dimly lit now, most of the candles having been snuffed out, some burned into the holders and extinguished themselves.

"After you." I opened the door for Jeoffry and motioned him through.

"For what it's worth Mattes, I have no idea what will happen." He said softly to me, stopping beside me as he walked through the door. "But I do know that you and your friends are stronger than you're ready to believe."

"You keep saying we're so powerful." I said back to him softly, my voice almost cold. "What of it! Where was it tonight? Where was it in the circle?"

He kept walking past me, without another word, and I followed him through the door, closing it behind me. When he dropped me off at a door, I said "You never answered my question."

"It's an answer you must find for yourself, Matthias." He disappeared through the next door down and left me standing there.

"Thanks." I said into the empty hall.

I went inside my room and saw Kaila on the bed, laying on her back, the covers pulled up to her waist. "I was wondering when you'd come to your senses. How are you, Mattes?"

"I'm fine, really." I pulled off my shoes and shirt and crawled under the covers. She stared at me, disbelieving. "Really." I promised her, brushing her chin with my fingers and kissing her lightly.

"Something is bothering you, Mattes. What is it?"

I was quiet for a second, not sure how to answer. "Look, Kaila—I've dragged you into my life and I'm sorry. Stuff like what happened tonight, it happens all the time around us. We're not very popular with some people. I would understand if you—"

"Listen to me Mattes, the only thing I'm afraid of, is losing you right now." She whispered. "Promise me to keep yourself alive, and put my only fear to rest."

"I can't promise that Kaila."

"Then promise me you'll stop worrying about me, and worry only about keeping yourself safe."

"I'll always worry for you Kaila."

"Just promise, Mattes."

I looked at her, my arm resting on my hand, and I could see the worry in the pale features of her face. "I promise," I told her then. "To try not to worry about you."

"Thank you." She said, kissing me softly. I wrapped my arms around her, holding her tightly, and kissed her back, loving the way she felt next to me.

We fell asleep like that, in each others arms. The light of the Sun came all too soon, peaking through the windows and caressing my face, waking me from a surprisingly good night's sleep. I stretched my arms and legs, untangling myself from the bed sheet and stepping out of bed. The ray of light cast through the window splayed a square patch on my side of the bed and off onto the floor.

I grabbed my shirt from the floor, it had been sitting in the direct light of the sun for some time, and felt warm on my skin as it slid over my back and settled. "Are you sure Jeoffry healed your ribs?" Kaila was awake.

"Positive." I said brightly.

"Maybe he could do something about that bruise." She trailed her speech.

"Kaila, I'm fine, I promise." I quelled her.

"One day Matthias, you're going to be badly hurt," her face looked kind of pouty, like a child begging for a chocolate chip cooking before dinner. "And you're going to say that you're fine, and you won't be."

"If I'm ever hurt that badly, I want you to run like you've never ran before, and get as far away as possible." I tried to make my expression hard, my eyes cold, when I said it, wanting to make sure she understood exactly how serious I was.

"Remember your promise, Mattes." She made it a statement, a soft reminder and I tried to quell that fear. "You have still never explained why your life is in constant danger, I think it's only right that I know."

"Kaila, I—" I didn't know where to begin or how to start. I stayed quiet for a moment, gathering my thoughts. Then I told her everything from the beginning; how my parents abandoned me, and how Maerik found me. I explained the night we received our Rites as clearly as I could.

"We noticed them seconds before anyone else," I hated

reliving this moment, hated the pain and the fear and the hate it wrought within me. "My Master, Maerik, died in my arms. He died protecting me and he told us to run. The spell we tried to use to get us away from there didn't work quite as expected and well, here we are."

"Mattes," She whispered. "I'm so sorry. You're the Chosen Ones then?"

"Don't be sorry." I told her. "He died saving our lives, I won't waste what he's given me. Besides, if I succeed, Maerik can live again in our own time. They all can. And yes, we're the Chosen Ones, or whatever you call it."

"Will you return, to where it is you're from, then?"

"I don't think I will, nor that I can."

"You got here, didn't you? Why is there any reason you can't go back?"

"Because we don't know how we got here in the first place, well not exactly. They had us trapped in their own dark spell when we cast ours, somehow their majick interfered with our own."

"It must torment you, to know that you are fighting to save

a time and place and people you will never get to see again. For that, I am truly sorry."

"I have you here, and that is all I'll ever need." I kissed her on the forehead to place emphasis on the fact.

"Are you two decent?" Kai called, rapping on the door a few times.

"You're an ass Kai." I said back. "You know better."

He opened the door slowly, peeking around the crack, as if to make sure he wasn't walking into anything. I knew he was just screwing around, and I guess I kinda deserved it, but it still irritated me. He pranced in and left the door open.

"Jeoffry asked me to come see if you guys are ready. Our boat will be here soon." Kai told us.

"As ready as I'll get." I said.

"Great, your packs are in the hall." I looked at Kai quizzically for his plural use of the word "Pack" and he continued quickly, explaining. "Jeoffry said you wouldn't mind Kaila, he got us all up at the crack of dawn to go out and get backpacks and supplies. We don't have horses to carry our crap anymore. Oh, and if you two aren't going to do it, then

I'm sleeping with you next time, I like the getting-to-sleep-in perk."

"Kai!" I yelled at him. Kaila blushed a light pink, a charming contrast to her generally pale, white skin.

"I'll be sure to give him my thanks." Kaila said, touching my arm letting me know it was okay and that I shouldn't kill Kai.

"I guess we should get going?" I asked.

"Probably." Kai answered. "Because I'm only getting started on my revenge. The longer I stand here, the better I can think of ways to torment you."

We followed Kai out the door and each took one of the three burlap sacks stretched over some wooden poles and swung them over our backs, letting the ropes rest on our shoulders. Jeoffry was sitting with Mica at a table in the dining area. When they saw us they stood and hoisted the packs leaning against the table legs over their shoulders and walked over to us.

"I was afraid you two would sleep all day." Jeoffry said.

"I would have if the windows had shades." I explained to

him. "We were up for a bit, actually, talking."

"Oh?" Mica said, a curious lilt in his tone.

"'Oh' nothing." I said with those little finger quotes. "Let's just get going."

We left, following Jeoffry in the direction of the river and eventually to a long wharf stretching a good distance out into the river, where it branched off all over the place. Ship masts polluted the view over the river and smaller boats cluttered the water.

It took us a while to figure out where we were supposed to be going, trying to navigate the docks was one thing, doing so without a clue as to which way to go was something else entirely on it's own. Thankfully we me met a deck hand who was able to show us the right way, which was in the direction opposite the one we were going. Convenient as always.

The deckhand led us through the maze that made up the wharf and out onto a large platform at the end of one of the docks where a mass of people were running around, tying ropes to the piles that extended above the deck. Jeoffry led us up a narrow, rigged plank onto the main deck of the ship where we were greeted by a steward of sorts. He was dressed better than the men securing the ship below and he held a roll of paper which he consulted when he addressed Jeoffry.

"Your name, sir?" He inquired.

"Jeoffry, I left a note with the dock master a few days ago requesting a suite on this ship to Schötre." Jeoffry pointed at the scroll before continuing. "Here I am, Jeoffry of Michval."

"Oh, of course. This way, my Lord." He started off at a leisurely pace, leading us down the pine planked top deck. He took us through a hatch and down a set of stairs into a narrow hall lined with doors and candle sconces that lit the area softly. He stopped at the very end of the hall, a single door was framed by this wall. "Ah, here we are, my Lord. If you need anything, you have but to ask."

When he was gone, and we were inside what must be a massive room for a ship this size with four doors leading presumably to other rooms, I turned to Jeoffry. "He didn't look like a sailor. Didn't sound like one either."

"He was probably just the ship's steward, he handles the

books and deals with the people. Most likely he's better educated than most of the sailors you'll meet. Not that they're not intelligent men," He pointed out. "Just not as educated as some in the subtleties of our language. Kaila, you'll forgive me, but had I known you would be coming I would have gotten an extra room."

"I was already going to Schötre, I have a room reserved." She explained.

"You're welcome to stay with me if you want." I told her. "This looks more comfortable than the other rooms this thing would have." Kai grinned and winked subtly at me and I politely flipped him off behind Jeoffry's back so Kaila wouldn't see.

"Well, I suppose you could be right." She said, pondering my offer. "You know what, why not. I'm sure it's much more comfortable in here than anywhere else on this thing. It would be nice to have some company too."

"Of course," Kai mumbled, a cocky grin on his lips. "Company."

I was sure to give Kai my best "I'll kill you later." glare, and put my arm over Kaila's shoulder, drawing her close to me. "I think Kaila and I will have the one over there."

As we started over to our room, when we were just a few fee from the door, Kaila looked up at me and asked softly, "Is your friend stupid, or does he think I'm deaf?"

"Stupid." Was my single word reply as we reached the door to our room and opened it, going through. The rooms was decorated in the same fashion as the common area. A plain writing desk sat against the wall adjacent to the door, a chair made of the same wood tucked underneath. The bed was just big enough for the two of us, and I noticed it was bolted to the floor, and upon closer inspection, I realized the desk was too. I assumed it had more to do with the boat rocking than the fear of unruly tenants.

Even while the boat sat stagnant in the water, I could still feel the gentle rocking back and forth as small waves and the natural current of the river gently moved the docked vessel. "I need to go talk to Jeoffry for a second, are you okay to get settled?" I asked Kaila, dropping my pack to the floor beside the bed.

"I'm not completely helpless., Mattes." She said, and

reached up and kissed me quickly.

"I'll be right back." I promised. I could only guess which room was Jeoffry's, so I went to the first of two rooms on the wall to my right and went through. Kai was moving about the room, putting the few pieces of clothing into a single dresser drawer. "What room is Jeoffry in?"

He jumped a bit, startled. "I didn't hear you knock."

"I didn't." I quipped.

"Of course." He said, sighing. "Pretty sure he got the one across from you. Are you pissed at me or something?"

"Well, it's not like you take every opportunity to imply that Kaila and I are screwing like a couple of horny-as-hell bunnies in the spring, or anything like that." I explained.

"Remember when we were in the car dealer's parking lot, and I told you I'd get you back?"

"Yeah...."

"Good." Was all he said.

It took me a second, and then I understood. "So that's what you're on about? Fine, so be it, I deserve it. But try to keep it away from Kaila. She's not dumb, or deaf. She heard you're little remark earlier."

"Fine, I'll leave her out of it, but I'm no where near done with you yet." He smiled wickedly at me.

I left him to whatever it was that he was doing, because it wasn't really worth calling it unpacking given we had so very little to unpack. I skipped the next door, and walked over to the door opposite mine and opened it up. The hinges creaked a bit, which I thought was strange because the ones on Kai's and my own were soundless. Shoddy maintenance crew I guessed and opened the door the rest of the way.

Kai was right, Jeoffry was in here, but so was Mica. They were both sitting on his bed, apparently previously talking but now waiting to see who it was on the other side of the door when they heard it start to squeak open. "What are you two up to?"

"Just talking." Mica said.

"Shouldn't you be unpacking or something?" I asked Mica.

"There's nothing to unpack really, what's the point?" He said it like it was obvious. It was. "Oh...if you want me to leave...."

"No," I sighed. "Stay, I just have a quick question for Jeoffry here."

"And I'm sure I have a quick answer." He said back.

"Not likely." I scowled. "Are you trying to get me and Kaila in bed?"

"I have no idea what you're talking about." He said, sounding slightly hurt at my accusation.

"You know damn well what I'm talking about." I told him, closing the door. "You and I both know that you didn't go down to see the dock master for the room until after you found out about Kaila."

"Oh." Was all he managed.

"Oh? Just 'Oh,' nothing else?" I said a little more heatedly.

"Okay, yes, I did go to the dock master after you met Kaila, but I didn't get a four room suite for the same reasons you think I did." He explained. "I thought you might want to be able to have some time alone with each other, without the rest of us, Kai especially, around. And I figured if you two wanted to, you know, whatever, you should be able to without sneaking around a bit. We might not win, Mattes. You of all people should understand that, I figured you would want to make the most of the time you have with her."

"Oh." Was all I managed.

"Oh? Just 'Oh,' nothing else?" Jeoffry mocked me.

"Thank you?" I said, trailing off the last word.

"You're welcome." He smiled a little bit when he said it, he also looked a little smug.

I rolled my eyes at him and went back to my room where Kaila was waiting for me. He had pulled the chair away from the desk and was sitting on it. Our packs were both nowhere to be seen, she probably emptied them into the dresser drawers like Kai had. "You unpacked, didn't you?"

"What's to unpack, there's hardly anything there, I just stuffed the packs into the drawers to get them out of the way." She stood up and walked over to me, putting her arms around my neck. "Yours is in the top drawer."

I leaned down a little and kissed her softly on the lips, and started thinking aloud. "I wonder how long it takes to get to

Schötre from here."

"A week at the most, if the wind is bad." She said, then she pulled away from me slightly. "Have you noticed that both times Jeoffry has made the lodging arrangements, we have both had to share a room."

"Well, you did say you had one reserved." I started.

"I'm not complaining, she said, I just find it odd, don't you?" She asked me.

"Well, yes, I mean no, I mean I did until I went over and asked him about it."

"Really? Whatever did he say?"

"He thought we might like some privacy away from them, and Kai. And—" I caught myself, but a little too late. I didn't really want to tell her the last part.

"And?"

"And nothing, that was all." I said.

"It was not, you were about to say something else, what was it?"

"Nothing, I swear."

"You're lying to me Mattes. Just tell me." There was a touch of warning in her voice, like if I didn't tell her, there would be consequences.

"And he thought that if we decided to, you know, we shouldn't have to sneak around to, well, you know." I could feel my face getting red, I was blushing. "He also said we might not win, and that I should relish every moment I have with you."

"I see." Was all she said, some color creeping up her neck.

"I didn't want to tell you that part." I mumbled.

"No, Mattes, we're being silly, he's right."

"He is?"

"Of course, I like being alone with you, it's peaceful and it feels right, you know?" She sat down on the bed, and I sat beside her. "I just thought that you had asked Jeoffry to, well, you know."

"I'm not like that Kaila, I've never even...."

"You've never..." And then she actually giggled at me me

for a second before catching herself and regaining her composure. "Really? Not even once?"

"No, have you?" I was curious now that she had started this conversation.

"It's not important." She said, closing the door on the topic. "Let's just enjoy every second with have with each other., like you said, you could fail."

"I can't. The world can't afford for us to fail." I told her.

"Don't be a hero, Matthias."

"I don't want to be a hero," I breathed. "Just Marqus' worst nightmare."

"I love you, Matthias." She whispered to me before moving closer to me and stretching up to give me a kiss.

"I love you too." I kissed her back.

"Bad time?" Kai said, standing in the doorway.

We jumped, startled, and looked at him. "What's up?" I asked him, brushing the back of my hand over my mouth.

"There's some food out here if you're hungry, since you two slept in I thought you might be." Kai explained his intrusion. "Its not great food, but it's food all the same."

"I'm in, we did skip breakfast." I stood, and walked into the common area, brushing past Kai and I could hear Kaila coming behind me.

The small, round table that was just large enough to fit the five of us, a small pot of steaming stew, five bowls, and a loaf of stale bread, like the bed and desk was anchored to the floor. I sat down with my back to the wall the main door was on, and Kaila sat down to my right, closer to our bedroom door. Jeoffry took the chair across from me with Mica and Kai on his left and right, respectfully.

"So, what's good?" I asked.

"Don't get your hopes up." Jeoffry said, making a face. "Food on these boats is never that good."

"Better than starving." I pointed out. "And besides, at least it's hot, it's already better than the crap we ate on the trail."

"You just haven't tasted it yet." Jeoffry explained.

"It can't be that bad." I ladled some of the steaming soup into the wooden bowl in front of me. The soup was lumpy and almost gray. It plopped loudly into the bowl, thick and heavy.

"Okay, it looks terrible, but I'm sure it tastes great."

While the soup or stew or chowder or something else entirely was hot, the flavor was terrible. It was almost like eating bland cardboard that was let to simmer over night in some hot water. The texture was about the same. "Could use some salt." I managed to choke out through a bite of the stuff.

"I'm sticking to the bread." Kai announced. "Did you want some more, er, whatever this is Mattes?"

"I'm good. I think I'll have some bread as well." I pushed back my bowl of garbage and grabbed a chunk of bread off the table.

"So, how long are stuck on this boat again?" Mica asked.

"A week at the most." I answered him, looking at Kaila in confirmation who nodded and took a chunk of bread for herself.

There was a few loud knocks on the door to the commons and I jumped about a mile, not expecting anyone to be knocking, we weren't expecting anyone, and I guess I could attribute it partially to my nerves being kinda shot given recent events. I had to remind myself though that anyone who was

262

interested in killing us would probably not be knocking on the door. Kai stood up and walked over, his shoes making a soft padding on the floor, and on the other side was the ship's steward.

"The captain has given the order to raise anchor. We should be moving momentarily. He's asked me to ask everyone to stay in their cabins until after we're out of the docks." The steward explained.

"We'll be sure to do just that." Jeoffry assured him. "Care for some soup?"

"Oh heavens no." The man said, cringing his nose. "I wouldn't touch the stuff with a ten foot pole. My advice, stick to the bread."

"Is there nothing else to eat?" I asked him.

"We have some fruit for breakfast, the food gets marginally better later." He explained.

"I see." I said.

"Well, this was my first stop, I have to continue on to the other cabins." He bowed himself out of the room, Kai closing the door behind him and taking his place at the table again, continuing to work on the chunk of bread he'd pulled from the loaf.

"I still say that steward guy is weird. He doesn't talk like anyone else I met on the ship or by the docks." I said to anyone who was listening. "Come to think of it, I didn't see anyone else on the ship but him."

"Mattes, quit being paranoid." Kai told me.

"He's not your typical steward, I'll give you that, but still." Jeoffry was breaking up a chunk of bread into bite-sized pieces, popping one into his mouth and chewing on it while he went about tearing the bread into smaller pieces. When there was nothing left but a pile of bread chunks, he brushed his hands together to get rid of the crumbs and went on. "I'm pretty sure he's harmless. He seems friendly enough, he even gave us good food advice."

"Let's just wait and see, shall we? If he means you harm, you'll know soon enough, otherwise we'll be off this boat in a few days time." Kaila spoke up, making a valid point. It's not like we could ask him if he is a bad guy, we'll find out either way soon enough.

Dinner was much better that night, corn on the cob, there was unfortunately no butter but it was sweet and delicious all the same. A small plate of baked potatoes, and some small steaks were served. Jeoffry explained that the food wouldn't always be this good since the ship had no way to store food for extended periods of time. I only hoped that we never had to see that gray gunk again.

After two days stuck in our cabin, conversation having run completely dry, I decided to venture topside to stretch my legs and get some air. It was dark, the darkness blanketing the river banks, shadows jutting across the deck of the ship and out onto the water.

It never stopped amazing me how many stars there were. It's not that more stars existed in this time, but more so that there was almost no light pollution here. Stars covered the sky, blocked only by the occasional drifting cloud. The steady night breeze played with my growing hair, still in need of being hacked off. I decided to find some scissors and cut it as best as I could when I got back to the cabin.

I hadn't been walking long, I had hardly reached the bow, when I heard voices talking in a loud hush. It was the sound of parents arguing in the night and trying not to wake the kids. I couldn't help but creep closer, to try and hear what the voices were saying. This must have been the captain's cabin, but who would be arguing with him in the middle of the night, and what about?

"Ye did nah say nuthin' 'bout murder." I could pick up his accent through his harsh, whispered growl. I presumed he was the captain.

"Our plans have changed, mage." I heard a voice I would recognize anywhere. Except it was colder, darker, scarier. This voice was tainted, eager, the voice of a madman. I knew the steward was a bad guy, and now I could prove it. "He won't be happy if we bring along the other two, and we can't kill them without drawing attention to ourselves, so they'll all have die."

"An' this be murder. I'll have nah a part o' it!" The older voice, the captain, exclaimed quietly.

"You'll do as you're told, or you can share their fate." The steward told him.

"An' who be doin' the deed then? Eh? If ye kill me." The

266

captain asked him.

"If they get away, what I do to you will feel like a mere tickle compared to what he will do to you." The steward cautioned.

I had left my mind open, letting Mica and Kai hear what I was hearing. This left me slightly distracted and when I tried to put my hand against the wall to lean closer, I accidentally leaned on a small stack of empty crates and they fell. I cursed at myself mentally, turned around and ran back in the direction of our cabin. Stuff like this was only supposed to happen in cheap horror movies.

I rounded the corner, stumbled, regained my step, and flew down the stairs to the cabin area and plowed through the door to our cabin, panting, out of breath. "I told you that guy didn't seem right."

"Right now is not the time for 'I told you so.'" Mica cautioned. "We need a plan or something, and quickly too."

"They must know someone was outside, overhearing everything." Jeoffry said.

"They won't come now, they know we would be expecting

them." Mica talked like he was thinking out loud. "No, they'll try to catch us off guard."

"Maybe they'll think it was just the rocking of the ship that knocked the crates over." I crossed my fingers.

"We still need to plan for the worst." Kai made a good point, letting our guard down now would just allow us to play into their trap.

"Well, what do we know?" I asked them. "He called the captain a mage, but they would have no use for him if the steward were a majician."

"Did you see either of their faces?" Jeoffry asked me.

"Well, no, but they were in a little cabin on the top deck, that has to be the captain's quarters, right? And the other guy had a real thick sailor's accent." I explained my reasoning. "Right guys?"

The other two nodded their heads in agreement and Jeoffry went on. "Right. He could be the captain. What of the Steward? From what I've heard, he could be our weakness. It seems that the captain is this guy's pawn. But why not just send a majician instead of going to the trouble to find a ship captained by one?"

"He needed someone he could trust." Mica said, after a brief silence between us, like he was having some grand epiphany. "And he didn't want to sacrifice another majician."

"That's it!" I said, understanding. "Marqus won't have any kind of lesser majicians laying around. He's only after the best, the most powerful. We keep besting every attempt he makes to capture or kill us."

"He needed someone disposable, someone who's death would be trivial if he failed again." Kaila said this, and I looked at her, she hadn't spoken until just now and I was caught off guard.

"He's completely changed his strategy." Kai said softly, oblivious to Kaila and her comment.

"What was the original plan then?" I wondered.

"Sail past Schötre and near the pass into Drät." Jeoffry said it like it was obvious, and it was, to anyone who knew the topography of the region. "Drug us and carry us into Drät."

"Wait, drug us? That must mean that the captain is a lesser alchemist." I said. "And not the captain, but the ship's doctor."

Mica was rubbing his temples, and shaking his head, laughing a little bit. "Oh my God. This is some God damn Jerry Springer shit. The motive changes more than I breathe and the doctor is cheating on the captain with the bad guys. You guys, we're plotting against a wannabe bad-ass with no exceptional abilities and an old man with minor herb majick."

"He has a point." Kai said. "Either we should go up there and just start shooting, or be afraid because there might be more than we know going on here."

"This is a plan created by a man who has sent us a demon care package and soulless men." Mica went on picking up on Kai's thought. "If what we know is true, then this is the stupidest plan to capture or kill someone ever, and honestly you guys, I'm feeling kinda let down here. I mean, I expected something a little more elaborate."

"How about we just ask them?" I asked sarcastically.

"Given the state of things, that's not a bad idea." I glared at Mica. "Oh, you were being sarcastic, still though, just sayin'."

"We factored out the steward too quickly." I said. "There has to be more to him than meets the eye, he's probably not a majician, but he's obviously scary enough to keep a leash on the cook."

"So we need to watch out for the food and keep our fingers away from the stewards mouth." Kai said.

"Jokes are over Mica, back to being big boys." I told him.

"You're always so serious these days." Kai said grudgingly.

"Somebody has to be." I grumbled.

"Ladies!" Kaila said too loudly. "Play nice."

We sat there, thinking quietly for a moment, no one saying anything, only cloth rubbing together or someone shifting in their seat filled the silence. "I'll sneak up to the doctor's cabin tonight, after we're sure the steward is sleeping."

"You can't, Mattes, it's dangerous." Kaila said in a hushed tone.

"I can, and he's a doctor and a feeble alchemist, I have nothing to fear from him, but if he knows what's good for him, he'll tell me what he knows about the steward." I said.

"And what if the steward catches you up there with the doctor?" Jeoffry asked me.

I thought for a moment, and answered him. "I'm looking for some ginger to calm my stomach, I'm not used to ships. That's innocuous enough."

"Fine, but don't get caught, and keep Mica and Kai informed of everything." Jeoffry said.

We spent the next several hours mostly silent, occasionally someone would make a suggestion or offer some advice which I noted in silence. It was torture waiting, a second was a minute, a minute, an hour, an hour a day. Time ground on slowly, and I grew more anxious every second, finally standing and pacing around the room coming back to my seat and getting up a second later to pace some more.

"It's time." Jeoffry announced when I thought I would go insane from a cruel combination of anxiety, anticipation, and impatience.

I walked briskly to Kaila and kissed her. "See you in a minute." Without waiting for a response, I went to the door and opened it, pulling it closed behind me and working my way down the hall, listening for footsteps ahead. I was hoping not to be seen by anyone, but if I was I had to act nonchalant and stick to my needing ginger for my stomach story.

When I got to the portal or doorway thing to the deck, I peeked my head up and peered around and didn't see anyone. I opened my mind completely to Mica and Kai and went up and onto the deck of the ship, retracing the steps I took earlier. It was eerily quiet up here at this time, only the water breaking against the ship's hull and churning in its wake made any sound.

My heart was pounding in my ears, adrenaline pumping through my veins. The closer I got to the doctor's cabin, the faster my pulse raced. When I was halfway there, I heard someone's boots padding across the deck, making hollow thumping sounds. My chest might have exploded, I don't know. I looked around quickly, hoping to find some place to hide.

I spotted a wooden crate holding more rope than anyone would possibly need spooled up into a giant coil. Beside it was a bank of ropes, tied off in complicated knots to metal anvil-like studs bolted to the mast and deck. I ducked into the rope bank, the box blocking the view with my back to the mast, the shadow cast by the sail hopefully completely hiding me from view.

The sailor walked right past me, whistling. When he was gone, I let out an audible sigh of relief and took a deep calming breath and let it go, letting my pulse settle to a calmer rhythm before setting off down the deck again.

I came to the spot where I was earlier, the crates were moved, and circled around to find a door. It was on the side facing the end of the ship, the handle a simple metal loop attached vertically to the door, with a small latch above to keep it closed.

The locking bar creaked softly as the tiny metal bar scraped against the latch as it lifted and the door squeaked open. "Who's there? Oh, who are ye? Ye startled me." There was a hint of panic in his voice.

"You thought I was someone else, didn't you?" I asked quietly closing the door carefully so as not to make too much noise. "Afraid the steward might pay you a late night visit, make sure you're behaving yourself?"

"What do ye wan from me lad?" The man asked, sitting back in his chair, relaxing.

"Let's start with the reason you're so scared of the steward, a man like yourself, possessing an arcane gift, should have nothing to fear from him." I said, taking a few steps closer to him, before bending and whispering softly in his ear. "What is his secret?"

"There be no secret lad, he be but a steward. Nothing to fear at all." The man said, I could see his throat working, swallowing anxiously.

"I know you two are up to something, I overheard the two of you talking earlier today." I told him, taking the arms of his chair in my hands. "And you're not waiting up for the tooth fairy."

"Ye don know what yer talkin' 'bout." He said quietly, softly, afraid.

I kept my face level with his, staring right into his eyes. I let my majick flow through me, emanate from me, let it seep through my pores, I let him feel the power as it arced from my skin to brush his own. I spoke softly, quietly, harshly. "I don't know what he can do to you to keep your lips sealed so tightly. But I can promise you this; whatever it is he might be able to do to you, if you don't tell me exactly what I want to know, I'll make the damn steward look like a teddy bear and anything he might do will be like a walk in the freaking park compared to me and what I'm prepared to do."

A fine bead of sweat broke on his forehead and his breathing came more quickly and more shallow. His adams apple bobbing up and down with his swallowing. "W-what do ye wan' from me lad. I'm just an old man, a physician, I know nothin' o what yer talkin' 'bout."

I stared at him, I didn't blink, I didn't move. I stood there, bent over, my hands on the arms of his chair, my eyes locked on the pupils contained inside those deep blue irises. I stood like that for a good ten seconds. "You know what I want, exactly what I want."

"Bu' the shade, if 'e finds out 'e'll kill me lad, 'e'll kill me." He said, his voice quivering.

"That's all I wanted to know." I told him, straightening up. "If anyone asks, I came looking for ginger to settle my stomach."

"Yer not goin' teh kill me?" He asked me. I didn't say anything as I turned and walked to the door.

"No." I said with my back to him and my hand on the door. I stood there for a second, thinking, and then opened the door, but before I left I looked back at him. "But if you oppose us when the time comes, your fate will be death."

I wondered if the events in this time have made me cold, a monster. I could remember a time when the faces of the lives I'd taken, destroyed, would flash around in my mind. A time when I could say finitely and with certainty the number of lives I'd stolen out of necessity, survival. Just moments before, I had stood in front of an innocent, and threatened his life with cold certainty.

The question of my humanity was an effervescent thought, continuously bubbling to the front of my thoughts. I kept wondering how I was any better than the people I stood to destroy, even my destiny was bent around destroying things, people. How does this not make me some kind of monster, some terror. Soon I was questioning my own sanity, and everything about me. This sense of dread creeping over me, the way spilled wine slowly stains a carpet, so was my conscious, my being, stained by this sense of horror at what I was becoming, what I had become. I wanted to jump over the banister on my right, just ten brisk steps and an easy bound and I would be free, I could swim to shore and disappear into the night. Leave my destiny and everything behind me.

Mattes, shut up. Mica called out to me.

You're such a drama queen. Kai said with a exaggerated amount of exasperation in his tone.

You've only done what you've been forced to do. Mica said to me. *It's not your fault that people had to die. Their blood rests on Marqus' shoulders.*

Look, just get back here, okay? Kai said, but then his tone became more serious. *Marqus is toying with your humanity, if anything this means you're a good guy. Monsters don't ask themselves if they're monsters.*

I guess it's appropriate that I don't believe you then. I said, a matter-of-fact tone touching my thought.

I was back at the hatch leading below deck to the cabins before I even realized it, my thoughts were so scattered and chaotic. I went down the steps, feeling kind of distant, detached. I knew I was moving, but I couldn't remember ever telling my body to move, I was just moving while my brain jumped from thought to thought, a montage flickering through my head.

When I was back in front of the door to our cabin, I forced my mind to settle so I could think coherently again and opened it. Kaila was at the table, her chair turned around to face me. I the others sat around the other side of the table so that the door was in front of them.

"So." I said brightly. "For those of you who aren't stalking my brain, the steward is a shade."Jeoffry's face paled, Kaila gasped slightly, and the other two sat there almost indifferent.

"Where in the hell did he manage to find a shade, let alone one willing to do his dirty work?" Jeoffry asked.

"More importantly, how in the fuck are we going to kill it?" I asked.

"You're not." The doctor was standing in the door. My body tensed, I turned on the balls of my feet and felt the majick flow through me, ready. "That will be enough, Matthias. Settle yourself."

"I thought I warned you, old man, do not stand against us." I said to him, my tone flat and cold.

"Ergo inter nos pax." He spoke in Latin, making his statement a contract of sorts between us.

"Esto." I said, relaxing, all but Kaila echoing me.

He offered his forearm to me, to which I waved it away. "We don't have time for intricacies, I'll take you for your word."

"Who are you?" Mica asked him. "I don't think you've mentioned that yet."

"Indeed." He said. "To be fair, you never actually asked."

"Ever heard of introducing yourself?" Mica said back.

"Once you know my name, you may understand why I'm less than forthcoming with it." He spoke with some air of wisdom. "At any rate, it is something I will not say here, names carry with them power, and with mine comes a destiny."

"You couldn't be..." I said.

"Quiet!" He said, tossing his arm out, and literally stealing my breath momentarily so I couldn't speak. "Not here."

I gasped a couple of times after he lowered his arm, but quickly caught my breath. "So then." I spoke between the first few gulps of air. "What do we call you, and what about your accent?"

"Pick something, and the accent was just something I was trying out, it got boring quickly." He said coming in and closing the door. "We have to get you off this ship, before the shade knows what I'm up to, time is not necessarily in abundance."

"What would you suggest then?" Kai asked him. "That we jump and swim?"

"Well, it's not that far." I said.

"Actually I was thinking more along the lines of an emergency vessel." The cook said.

"They're bulky and clunky." Jeoffry protested. "They'll hear us before we hit the water."

"I have it sorted already." He assured. "We have but only to lower the vessel into the water, its been rigged up already."

"And then what? Drift aimlessly downstream?" I asked.

"Schötre is only a few hours out." He said.

"It feels too..." Mica struggled for the right word.

"Simple?" I postulated.

"Easy?" Kai ventured.

"Both." He said.

"I think perhaps we should be moving." The doctor said.

"We'll need to grab our packs." Jeoffry said and stood, going to his room. We all followed suit, Kaila pushed me back into my seat and went into our room and came out moments later with our packs, followed shortly by the others.

"Shall we?" The cook asked, taking the door handle and pulling the door open.

Framed in the door was the shade, he was making clicking noises with his tongue, like a mother clucking at a child who's about to be scolded. "I'd hoped I was wrong in thinking you couldn't be turned."

"Toth, you know better. Lucky I was right in thinking you could be fooled." The cook explained calmly, moving closer to us. "Your greed for power has always made you naïve."

"But this time Cian, my friend, you're not leaving alive." He stepped through the door and others garbed in black stepped through the door behind him, lining up against the wall. "You have nowhere to run."

"When that day truly comes Toth, you will rue it." Cian said, and Toth's face slackened for a second before he regained his serious composure, a menacing look burning behind his glare.

This wasn't exactly how I'd imagined finding Cian, but it beats not finding him at all. I had suspected he was Cian since he talked about names and their power, but I dropped the idea at his request. I guess it doesn't really matter much now though since the cat seems to have been let out of the bag, so to speak. Though which cat, and why the secrecy, I'm baffled.

"I still have a few tricks you don't know Toth." Cian said, grabbing my hand behind his back. I took the hint and grabbed Kaila's hand, and she took Kai's who latched onto Mica who obviously then took Jeoffry's. "One day though, I promise you, you'll have your wish. There will be no place to run and I will cleans this land of you."

Cian sounded so sure, so matter-of-fact, like he knew Toth

didn't stand a chance, and if that was the case, why wait, why not just destroy him here and now. Fear tainted Toth's face, I could see it creeping into his eyes and the slackness of his face. Cian squeezed my hand tightly, I held tighter to Kaila, not sure what he was planning, and lent him any energy I had to spare. He accepted it, and I felt his majick start to course through him, I could feel a power so great vibrating through his body.

"Libera nos domi." Cian said in a deep, thundering, rich voice that seemed to envelope you in it's folds and lilts as the words flowed from his lips. A ring of blue light, almost flame-like, surrounded us an blazed brighter and brighter until it was black, no one could see anything.

Prophecy

It was dark, and quiet and cramped. I let go of the hand I was holding. The only sound was shallow, labored breaths coming off the floor. I was scared at first. "Someone get a light." I said quickly.

Kai drew up a ball of fire from his hand, and lit the room. Cian was on the floor, curled up slightly, catching his breath like he'd had the wind knocked from him. "I'll—be—fine." He gasped out. "Just—need—to—breathe."

I scanned the room lit by the soft glow of Kai's flame and set each candle I saw alight, letting Kai lower his arm. When I was done, there was plenty of light, and you could see the old-world decor more clearly. A few tapestries hung from the

285

walls, and small ancient-looking instruments were strewn over the available shelf space, and scattered over the small coffee table surrounded by large fluffy looking cushions.

The room was actually quite larger than my initial impression in the dark. Huddled together in the dark, the room seemed extremely cramped. "Back up a bit, let him breathe. Mica, can you find us some water?" I asked.

He returned a little later with a goblet full of water. I took it from him and helped Cian sit up, and held the glass out to him. He took it and gulped it down, draining the last dregs of water and letting an audible sigh escape his lips. "How do you feel?"

"Oddly enough, I feel as though I transported six people over fifty miles or so by majick." Cian said.

"Oh, you're funny." Kai said.

"I try." He said, trying to stand. He was still a little unsteady and weak, so I caught him when he stumbled. I led him to the coffee table and helped him onto a large cushion with his back to the wall, and I put another cushion behind him and sat down.

"So," Mica leaned on the table. "How did you do it?"

"Do what?" Cian returned.

"You know," Kai said. "Take us from the boat to here, without passing out for a week, and actually going where you wanted to go."

"Ah." Cian said. "You three tried a similar piece of majick when you were attacked, did you not? And now you're wondering why you traveled back in time, and why I was able to achieve amicable results, no?"

"Well, yeah." I said. "But how do you know all that?"

"Suffice it to say I know everything there is to know of you three, I know of your past, your present, and of your destinies." Cian winked. "It comes with my being your prophet."

"So you did deliver our prophecy all those years ago." I said in disbelief. "You've aged well."

"Actually, I haven't." He said. "The physical process stopped when I received the Gift, and tonight it shall begin once more."

"You still haven't answered my question." Kai reminded.

"The answer is a simple one." He said. "And you already know it, you're just blind to the answer."

"What are you talking about."

"Remember, majick is guided more by your intent, your heart, than the words you channel it through." He explained. "You ought know that by now given your discovery of your elemental abilities. Incantations, and verbal majick are an invention of the post-Trinca era. Then, we only used words to guide the most difficult of majicks.

"When you worded your majick, your design was to go back to your house, but in your heart Matthias, your heart wanted nothing more than to have your teacher back, for everyone to be okay." Cian finished, his deep green eyes staring into my own, seemingly burrowing their way into my consciousness.

"So instead of going home, I took us to a place in time where we could stop the attack from happening." I was beginning to understand why all this was happening. "But why not just go back a few days or a few months, years even, why

288

so far."

"That I do not know, perhaps there is more for you to do here than save your future, perhaps you wanted to completely eradicate this rebel group, what you might call a 'coven.'" Cian explained.

"Maybe if you delivered the prophecy?" Mica asked him.

"Are you sure you want to hear it?" He asked solemnly. "You can refuse it, we choose our own destinies though, when I say I hold yours, I account only for one. Once you hear your prophecy, you must fulfill it, no matter the outcome, if you resist the prophecy will still be fulfilled, but with a greater chance of an undesirable outcome."

"Cian, I understand the risks, and I shall receive my destiny." I said to him.

He looked at me, resigned, and sighed. "So mote it be."

In times forgotten,
darkness is borne.
Hallowed ground,
poisoned by the Darkest.

Three from the future,
will join the last;
a forgotten race reborne.
My kiss for your race,
the stolen gift to be earned.
Earn your Rite,
to defeat the plight.

His eyes glowed a soft blue-white while his lips moved. I could feel the words move through me like some ancient power, they seeped through every ward I had protecting me. When the last word was spoken, I felt as though a great weight had settled over me, resting square on my shoulders until it slowly faded away.

"How much of that do you understand?" Cian asked us.

"The first part is rather simple, it's already happened. Marqus is the darkness who was born in times that have been forgotten   to everyone—" Kai said.

"Not everyone." Cian interrupted him. "I remember it well."

"So be it, but that's what the prophecy is talking about,

right?"

"I believe you are correct, yes." Cian said.

"And the second part, about the poisoned ground, it must mean Drät and the Darkest must be Marqus." I said.

"And 'three from the future,' that's a no-brainer." Mica carried on. "It's us."

"What does it mean by 'will join the last?'" I asked.

"You know the answer," Cian said. "Think carefully for a moment."

I thought about the next line, "a forgotten race reborne." Suddenly the light bulb went off and I said "It's you! Isn't it?"

"Very good." Cian said. "Yes, it is me, the last surviving Trincan, the last Elder."

"We're Trincan and we're to join you." Kai said. "I should have thought of that."

"You're much more than Trincan, child." Cian explained.

"The last four lines are still a mystery though." I said.

"I think you'll find that it's less of a mystery than you think."

291

Cian rebutted. "Think hard."

Mica kept repeating the last four lines, then he paused at "stolen gift" and started muttering the words to himself, over and over. "Mattes, that's it! Your dream!"

"Right, I said, the tree I saw, it mentioned a stolen gift!" I said, understanding.

"Tell me." Cian said, his voice hinting at urgency.

So I told him about the dream, how I saw Maerik, and then the tree, I told him what it told me, word for word. I told him of the power it radiated, of it's beauty. I explained in as much detail as possible, trying to do the being justice.

"The Elder Tree sought you out." Cian whispered. "That's never happened before. You must perform a dream quest to consult with the Elder Tree."

"The Elder Tree?" My tone made it a question.

"In a time long, long before my own, before the Elder came to be, in a time when it was just Trinca, our Mother, Ekydna, granted us the Elder Tree, a gift from her to our own race. It borne from our race the Elder, who formed the Elder Council and governed us." Cian explained. "Any Trincan could seek the council of the Elder Tree through a dream quest, during which your spirit passes through the Astral Gate. If you accept the ordeal, and survive it, you became Elder, and could sit on the council. Few dared to make the quest and fewer still accepted the ordeal. Only a small handful returned. Because so few were strong enough to pass the ordeal, the Elders received Ekydna's gift, immortality, living until such a time as another was able to take their place and sit on the council. Only then could they choose to live again."

"So we have to seek council with the Elder Tree and accept the ordeal." I said.

"You do." Cian said.

"What if we choose not to accept the ordeal?" Kai asked.

"You cannot." Cian said. "Remember, once you hear the prophecy, you cannot deny it."

"Fine," Mica said. "We'll do what we must. But what's this about the 'stolen gift?'"

"Marqus." I said, watching my thumbs circle each other in my lap. "He managed to steal the gift from Ekydna."

"You're half right." Cian said. "Marqus was once Elder, and

still believes himself to be Elder. He plotted the disappearances and later deaths of the Trincan council. When the last three of us who remained realized what he was doing, we attempted to retake what no longer belonged to him, bringing violence against your brethren was an unforgivable act. In the name of Ekydna we set to strip him of his Rite, but he fled into the mountains and hid in the endless caverns and caves there. Only a desolate man could commit his crime, and would never have passed the ordeal rightfully. It is believed he used some form of dark majick to assist him in deceiving the Elder Tree."

"Where did you disappear to before you gave the prophecy?" I asked him, remembering what Ephraim had told us.

"Marqus captured me, and was planning to kill me." Cian explained. "He tried for some time to convert me, but was unsuccessful. I managed to escape, but only just."

"How did he manage to capture you?" I asked him.

"Marqus found a way to dissolve the Gift, a dark poison." He said sadly. "My two companions who I had set out with to destroy Marqus became afflicted with the poison and died. He captured me while I was weak. Enough about the past, it's hardly important now."

"How do we return the gift to Ekydna and how do we become truly Elder then?" Mica asked him.

"The later is simple, perform a dream quest and seek council with the Elder Tree." Cian explained. "Until you fulfill your ordeal, you cannot learn how to perform the earlier."

"When you said earlier you would begin aging again today, that had nothing to do with you delivering the prophecy, and prophets living until their prophecy was delivered, did it?" I asked him.

"Yes and no." Cian said. "You see, I had to deliver the prophecy in order for you to understand what you must do. And you must become Elder so that I can finally, after too many centuries, begin to age and one day pass peacefully over into Ekydna's grace."

"So how do we start this dream quest?" Mica asked.

"You'll have to look inside yourselves for the answer, deep inside, if you catch my meaning." Cian winked at me.

I thought about what he said for a moment, thinking about

his meaning. Then I realized what he meant, and explained. "The answer must be in our cores, the way through the Gate."

"But there's only two paths, one to you and one to Kai." Mica said.

"We'll have to dig deeper." I explained. "Unless of course, you could be more specific?"

Cian gave me a knowing stare. "I cannot, you must discover this on your own, I've said all I can. Tea, Kaila?" He stood, walked around the small mahogany table, and went through a hole in the wall. It was covered by a thin, gray drape. Kaila followed him, and we were left alone, still sitting at the table.

"Shall we?" I asked, moving over to an open spot on the floor, near where Cian had fallen when we arrived. The other two followed me over, and found spots on the hard floor, a thin area rug covering the maple floor boards.

I closed my eyes and cast myself out, building a protective circle around me, to protect my body while I was predisposed. I let my consciousness fill the little bubble I created for myself, testing its strength. When I was satisfied I sunk into myself, soon finding the bright ball of fiery light that was my core and the connected basins of blazing energy that swirled and spun in their metaphysical containers.

I saw the cords of energy connecting myself to the Mica and Kai. I let my heart and breathing slow to a point where they were barely functioning, and allowed myself to sink deeper into my core, I felt the blaze of energy as I passed through the very epicenter of my majick, it felt like flames licking my skin. The sensation slowly faded as I sunk deeper.

Inside was a chaotic mess of swirling energy, it was dizzying and disorienting. I tried to close my eyes to protect them from the brilliance and intensity of the light, but I had no eyes or eyelids with which to cover them. So I concentrated harder, allowing myself to focus and sink deeper into my power. At some point, the energy started to slow, to become more dull.

Eventually I was looking at a black abyss below and a soft glow reminiscent of the blazing light and energy that flows above. At the center of the darkness was a faint strand of light peaking through. I found that going deeper into my core was getting easier and easier with each passing moment. Soon

297

enough the light began to grow into an endless string out of some point in the dark and continued on indefinitely.

It was composed of the purest white light I'd every known, so perfectly white, and perilously thin, no where near as heavy looking as the connections to Mica and Kai. This must be what ties me to Earth, what keeps me alive. I remember being told that the balance between life and death is thin, I just never understood how thin.

Thinking this was the bridge through the Astral Gate, I fed my essence, my consciousness, onto the strand of power, moving along it slowly at first, feeding myself onto the cord like popcorn onto string. It felt like an eternity traveling along that thin cord of power, after some time, I thought to look behind me and saw nothing. Which, for whatever reason I found odd, but I couldn't remember why that should be, or what I wanted to see. I realized after a moment that what I found perturbing was the lack of the cord behind me as it was before me.

It took a moment for me to understand that this meant there was no way back, and I panicked before I realized it didn't matter, and I had to continue forward, since there was no other direction to go. So I went on, traveling down that path, wondering where I was going, how much longer before I was there, and what to expect when I got there.

My mind started to consider all the possible things I would have to do for my ordeal. Slay a dragon, face a fear, both since dragons could be scary, not that I would know having never met one. I had a manager once, at Dean's Diner, who probably could have passed as one, she didn't shoot fire from her nostrils but she probably could have if she tried.

Since everything was completely dark, I had no perception of time or how far I had gone or how fast I was going. I tried to speed up, to get to wherever it was this thread went, if not the Astral Gate, faster, but had no idea if I was actually moving any faster. Soon though, or I thought it was soon, a tiny pillar of light came into view. As time went on it grew, taller and wider. I guess this was that proverbial "light at the end of the tunnel." I'd always envisioned it as a circular portal, not the massive pillar of light it was growing into as I approached.

When I was inches away from the pillar, it loomed above me indefinitely. I couldn't decide if I should just wait here for someone to come get me, knock, or just continue on through.

After a second of considering the absolute absurdity of the idea of knocking, given it was light and I had no arms, and since the chances of someone popping out and welcoming me in were slim, I decided to just continue on through.

The light felt cool and hot and powerful all at the same time as I went through. Immediately I was in full human form again, greeted by a massive plain of silvery, wispy, ghostly grass that went on forever. There was no one else here, nothing but ghost-grass. I couldn't help but wonder where the giant tree from my dreams was, and where I would find it.

You'll find me when you're ready, child. The eerie, ominous voice rang in my head.

"I don't have time for this!" I yelled back into the silence. "Show yourself!"

Nothing. No reply came and I started walking, picking a direction and continuing forward, with each step I wondered if I was going the wrong way but kept telling myself that I would find it in just another minute, just another minute, just another minute. I must have reassured myself of the fact fifty times or more, before I started to become increasingly frustrated with all of this.

"Look." I yelled into the distant nothingness. "I didn't ask for this. I didn't ask to go back in time. I didn't ask to have some great destiny to save the world. I. Did. Not. Ask. For. This!" I yelled each word louder than the last, panting for air when I'd finished.

No. You didn't.

"Then why are you doing this to me?" I yelled back.

Because it is your destiny.

"I didn't ask for this God-damned destiny!" I screamed.

No, but you accepted it.

"Yeah, I did. I accepted my destiny. I vowed to destroy the darkest of the dark. I vowed to never turn to their side, and didn't, even when given an out, I chose to fight, to run. I chose the light, the good, I chose to help people."

Have you?

"Haven't you been listening to me?" I was on the verge of tears wrought from frustration. "I'm here so that I can fulfill your prophecy and destroy the Dark Grail, the ones who have brought so much pain and agony into my life."

301

Is it right to punish these men for the crimes their children committed? It asked me.

"No. But their own crimes warrant their deaths."

Are you any better Matthias, than the man you seek to destroy, have you not committed the same sins of murder?

"I have only done what I've done to protect those that I love. Not to gain more power to cause more destruction. 'To do a great deed you'll do a little wrong.'"

It will be another millennium before that phrase has any meaning.

"What does it matter?" I asked angrily. "At this rate, I'll still be here having this same pointless conversation."

That may be so.

"Look, we're wasting time like this. If you're not going to give me your gift, send me back." I yelled into the distance. "With or without your help I'm going after Marqus."

And surely you will perish.

"So be it then, I'll die." I Said, some of the anger dissipating from my voice, turning into sincerity. "I'll be no more dead than I would be if I'd never come here; at least this time, perhaps I'll save a life."

Perhaps you will. You're brave child.

"And that, why do you keep calling me that, 'Child,' I'm not a damn kid!" I said, anger returning with my frustration.

I am ancient, and when you are ancient, I will be more so I have existed for longer than time, longer than this planet, since the beginning. You will always be a child.

"Will you do nothing but talk in circles?" There was silence for a brief period before something changed. I still have no idea what, but it felt almost physical and yet no at the same time. The sensation was weird, like someone was watching me.

When I turned around to see if I was alone, there it was. The great tree from my dreams was planted in the ground behind me. It towered over me, filling my view of the sky and sea of ghostly grass beyond.

It is my gift you seek, and my gift you shall believe, but tell me young-one, do you know what it truly is you seek?

"Your gift, your help, your blessing, anything to help me in

303

my efforts against Marqus. The prophecy says I can't do it without you, and that I must return the gift he stole from you." I explained.

All true, but do you understand truly of what you're asking? My gift you seek, and my gift you receive, but is it a curse or a blessing?

"I'm not sure what you mean?"

My gift is life, eternal life. You cannot die, doomed to walk this land for eternity.

"I thought I could give it up when another took my place?"

I fear there may be not be another. Is this truly what you want?

"Be it curse or blessing, I'll bear it as my cross, a small price to rid this world and land of the evil Marqus wields. I have a question though, how is immortality supposed to help me in my fight against Marqus?"

You cannot die, child, not until you're born.

"Until I'm born?"

You're in the past of your future, but you cannot exist with yourself. When you're born in the future, this part of you will cease to exist.

"So I will die one day? Even if I can't find others to sit on the council."

You will stop existing one day, yes. And the council? There will be no council as there was before, but for balance to be restored, it will one day exist in some new capacity.

"What do I have to do then?"

This is what you want?

"Yes."

So be it.

Everything changed. I was in the middle of a giant clearing, it looked so familiar, and yet so different. It reminded me so much of the Gathering ground back home. Someone was there, kneeling in the center on one knee, a sword in his hands pointed to the ground.

I felt a strange weight around my waist, resting on my hips, and looked down to see a heavy leather belt and a long scabbard hanging from it, the hilt of a magnificent sword protruding from the scabbard.

I could hear my hear speed up, could feel the sweat beading on my forehead. The person in the center of the clearing didn't move, didn't speak, they just stood there. My hand fell to my waist, clutching the hilt of the sword, which fit perfectly in my hand.

I took a step forward, craning my neck to try and get a better look at the figure. He looked familiar, like I knew him from somewhere, but that couldn't be, no one I knew could have followed me here. I took another few steps forward, until I was only a few feet away from this stranger.

"Who are you?" I asked.

"I think you know the answer already." The voice, the voice was my own. A wave of chills rand down my spine, the hair on my neck and arms standing on end, I still couldn't see his face, but my heart was speeding up and I knew what I would see before I saw it, but I didn't want to believe it.

"What—what are you?" I asked.

He raised his head slowly, and I could see my own eyes staring back at me. "I am your every folly, your every weakness, I am your darkest thoughts and memories. I am everything you fear, everything you hate about yourself. I'm you."

"Can you help me out of this place?" I asked.

"Only one of us will leave." He said.

"What?" I felt fear forming a lump in my throat. "We'll kill each other, we cannot fight."

"We can." He said, and instinctively I drew my sword. "And we will."

He was fast, standing and gripping his sword as he charged me a second later. He laughed insanely, gleefully as he charged and swung his sword over his head in a high arc that would end on top of my skull cap. I parried the strike and brought my sword around swinging at his left leg.

"Oh, we're good." He said smugly as he swung his blade down to block my own, continuing around in another arc, shorter, tighter than the last, aiming for my throat.

I blocked it easily and strafed left, levying a blow to his head which blocked and countered with another swing at my legs. "This is stupid." I said, swinging my sword down to protect my legs. The clash of swords rang in my ears, I could feel each blow vibrate down the shaft of the blade and into the hilt, vibrating and jerking my whole arm with the weight of each blow.

"That may be true he said," swinging his sword again as I spun around to block him. "But only one can leave this place."

"That's stupid." I grunted. "I need you as much as you need me. Without each other there is no balance. Even as much as I hate you, I need you."

He said nothing as he attacked again and again, each time I countered him and returned his strike, and he did the same. We were evenly matched, neither of us would win, or we would both die. "Why is it that you hate me, Mattes?"

"Because if it were not for you, Maerik would be alive, I would not be here, and we would be doing this." I said through my teeth as he blocked blow after blow.

"So kill me!" He yelled and renewed his frenzy, striking harder and harder, faster and faster.

I was beginning to weaken, the sword was growing heavy in my hands, my breaths were shallow and quick as we danced around each other trading futile blows back and forth.

"I can't!" I screamed at him. "And you know that as well as I do."

"Can't Mattes, or won't?" He asked me.

"Both." I said, fending off his latest series of blows.

We fought like this for what felt like hours, back and forth, neither of us gaining any ground over the other. Soon we were halfheartedly swinging our swords, the loud clanging of the blades now little more than a dull chink as they met each other. In one final effort, I swung my blade up as he cut across at my chest and caught his blade on my own, twisting mine around his and jerking against his thumb, his sword flew from his hands and landed out of sight in the trees beyond.

We stood there, panting, staring each other in the eyes, neither moving, neither speaking, until at last he said "Finish me."

"Never." I said, and threw my sword after his. "If only one can leave this place, then we'll leave together, as one being, as it is supposed to be."

"You're a fool" he said, and lunged at me. I wasn't

expecting him and his fist smashed into my face, shattering my nose. Pain spread across my face, radiating outward from the blow. Blood gushed from my nostrils, running in rivulets down my face, I could taste the strong metallic twang of blood in my mouth as I opened it to breath.

My eyes watered so badly I could barely see, but I found his blur and lunged at him, grabbing him up around the arms and holding onto to him as hard as I could, refusing to let go. He swung his head back and smashed it into my face, doubling the pain, black dots spotting my vision as I struggled to stay awake.

He swung his head back again and I tilted my head back, so he would miss me this time. "Stop!" I yelled at him. "Just stop! As much as I hate you I love you, we cannot exist apart. I won't fight you anymore."

He struggled a moment longer and fell still, becoming limp in my arms.

Wise beyond your years Matthias Boeing, you shall lead my Council well.

And then, there was darkness. I woke back in Cian's

sitting room, laying in my circle. I felt so weak and drained, like someone had beaten me with a sack full of blocks. I heard raised voices in another room, but I couldn't make out what they were saying. I rubbed out the circle and stood, but I became extremely light-headed and fell into the wall, knocking everything off the shelves that hung there. It crashed to the ground making some god-awful cacophony of noise making my head pound and throb, and my eyes water from the pain.

A second later the room was full, almost completely. But I didn't recognize anyone here. The room was silent, eerily so. They all looked as though they were in some form of awe. There was strange light illuminating the room, and then a sudden commotion broke the silence, as someone started pushing their way through everyone "Move it!"

"Get the hell out of my way!"

"Back your ass up." And there was Kai as he pushed a guy in light armor aside and broke through.

"Kai?" I asked. "Why is everyone in armor."

"Ask her." He said, his voice full of disgust as Kaila

appeared out of the mass.

"Kaila?" I asked her.

"Mattes." She sobbed lightly. "You're okay."

"Yes, I'm fine, but what's going on?" I asked her.

"You're glowing." Mica was here now, having found his way through the group crowding the room.

"Shut up!" Kai said to him. "Kaila, tell him. Now!"

"Tell me what?" I asked him.

No one said anything for a moment, there was only the collective sound of everyone breathing and the throbbing in my head that wouldn't cease. Kaila broke the silence whispering "Mattes, I'm sorry."

"Sorry for what?" I asked

"I'm." She sobbed. "I'm not who you think I am."

"What do you mean?" I asked her, becoming more alert, headache intact.

"I was sent by the King, Mattes." She started to explain. Her eyes were wet with fresh tears, more beautiful than I'd ever seen them.

"I thought you were in Ashara on business." I said.

"I was," she explained. "But my business was to find you."

"So you found me." I said, "What of it?"

"And kill you." She sobbed.

"And kill me? Kaila, what in the hell are you saying."

Her crying was making anything she said almost impossible to understand. The soldier in the front spoke then. "The Lady, was given the orders to destroy the Chosen should they fall to the Darkness."

"Kaila, you lied to me?" I asked her.

"It was my job. I had to." She cried.

"But I loved you?" I told her.

"And I you, Mattes. I still love you, I've loved you from the moment you ran me over. I didn't know who you were then Mattes. It was only later that I realized." She said.

"When did you find out?" I demanded.

"I didn't know until you told me in Ashara." She sobbed.

"And would you have killed me then?" I asked her.

She was quiet for some time. "I was afraid of that." I told her.

"You don't understand." She said.

"What don't I understand, Kaila?" I yelled. "That you lied to me, or that you would kill me as soon as look at me. You know what, save it. Where is Cian."

"He went outside shortly after we woke, to grab some preserves from the fruit cellar, but never returned." Mica explained. "I went out looking for him, but he's gone. There are his footsteps in the mud to the cellar, but none out, and he wasn't in the cellar at all."

"Are you sure?" I asked.

"Yes, Marqus must have him." Kai said. "I searched the cellar too. There were no false walls or hidden doors either that I could see."

"So now what?" I asked.

"You are to return with me upon the King's orders." The soldier in the lead said.

"Or what?" I said, beginning to crack up. "Will you kill me? Good luck there buddy."

"You have the gift?" He said, and then he bowed to one knee, putting his arm across his chest. "The Council has returned, and the Chosen have accepted their destiny."

"We have, and it has." I said. "What business is it of your King."

"Mattes, if not for me then for yourself. He has valuable information, decades of intelligence gathered on the Dark Grail. You need him as much as he needs you." Kaila explained. "Return with us."

"What of Cian?" I asked. "Who will save him?"

"He is nothing more than bait, Marqus will keep him alive to lure you to him." Kaila said. "But there are things you must learn first, things you must do. You can't fight this war alone, you need the help of the King and his army."

"Then we'll go, but Kaila, how can I trust you again?" I asked.

Coming Soon...

Kai's

Book

Acknowledgments

I conceived the idea for *Majician's Journey* while reading *Trickster's Queen* by Tamora Pierce in 2006. I've always loved writing and reading, but something she wrote, and to this day I can't remember what it was, in that book struck up some fierce emotion that caused some epiphany. The idea built and built as I took pen to paper and started creating each character, learning their fears and desires, their pasts and began to gain ideas of their futures. Tammy is an amazing woman and an even better author. Thanks for your inspiration, I hope I can someday return the favor and inspire another to create a great adventure for the world to enjoy.

Thank you for your advice and good-will, I will never forget it.

I think though, more importantly I need to mention Jo Rowling, when during a third grade class trip to the library, the librarian introduced us to the library and book selection, spending barely a moment on *Harry Potter*, citing that it would be an ambitious read for us. I've always been an ambitious person and welcomed the challenge. Jo, Thank you for sparking a fire inside of me that has evolved into a roaring bonfire, devouring every last drop of literature that falls into my hands. Thank you, thank you, thank you!

I think it's also fair to mention everyone who's ever had to put up with me in these four years, all of my whining when I had writer's block, my frustration and ranting when I decided to re-write a chapter, seven times, each time my computer crashed and I had to start re-typing my hand-written manuscript. However, a special thanks to Kim Young, Jessica Barton, Denae and Roger Workman, and everyone else; you guys and gals put up with me and offered suggestion after suggestion even after I put most of them down, you've helped more than you realize to discover the story I needed to tell.

Thanks to all the ladies and gentlemen at the Jeanette

Public Library, you've been amazing and have treated me so well over the years, I promise to come pay those late fees as soon as I donate a copy of this book to the collection.

A huge thanks goes to Mr. Kandella of West Hempfield Middle School; Bill Soff, Erica Schaffran, Mrs. Hepler of Hempfield Area Senior High School. You're all amazing educators and the best mentors of my life, having shown a genuine interest in me and my achievements and paved the road for what I have become. You represent the most unappreciated profession in our society and deserve so much more for what you do every day. Mr. Kandella of West Hempfield Area Middle School, thank you for taking a genuine interest in what I wrote, and for letting me be creative with my writing assignments. Bill and Erica, my thanks are endless to you both, no one else has challenged me and motivated me so well before, thank you for inspiring me to do better. Bill, a special thanks goes to you and the methods you use to teach your class, more could learn from it.

Mrs. Hepler, I can't say enough, you've been such a huge influence on me. Your monthly book discussions, accented with some of the best soups ever, kept me coming to school.

Thank you so much for showing me that reading can be a competitive sport, of sorts, and thanks to the Westmoreland Interscholastic Reading Competition for making that possible. Thank you for not noticing when I came to the library to help out so I could skive off Geometry. You've helped in ways words can't really describe, your demeanor and attitude were great, I've never met a teacher whose students enjoyed being around them more than you. I wish I could have visited before you retired.

Another thanks to my family for all their support, my mom and dad especially, without you, well I clearly wouldn't be here right now, but most of all thanks for giving me the best childhood you could, because it never lasts long enough.

And lastly, but certainly not least, a thanks to Paul Flere for his invaluable assistance with the cover of the book, you took what looked "OK" and made it exceptional. Thank you. And another thanks to all of my IRC friends over at irc.x10hosting.com you guys and gals have been great, helping with more than just literature (some of you really know how to save a programmer's life).

www.ingramcontent.com/pod-product-compliance
Lightning Source LLC
Chambersburg PA
CBHW062024170626
46813CB00001B/281